DRUGS IN
AMERICA

ISSUES FOR THE 90s

MANAGING TOXIC WASTES
by Michael Kronenwetter

THE POOR IN AMERICA
by Suzanne M. Coil

THE WAR ON TERRORISM
by Michael Kronenwetter

**MEDICAL ETHICS:
MORAL AND LEGAL CONFLICTS
IN HEALTH CARE**
by Daniel Jussim

DRUGS IN AMERICA
by Michael Kronenwetter

ISSUES FOR THE 90s

DRUGS IN AMERICA

The Users, the Suppliers,
the War on Drugs

Michael Kronenwetter

JULIAN MESSNER

Photo Acknowledgments

Pages 3, 79: AP/Wide World Photos. Page 18: Frank Fisher/Gamma-Liaison.
Pages 29, 108: UPI/Bettmann Archive. Page 35: Gatewood/The Image Works Inc.
Page 54: Greg Smith/Gamma-Liaison. Page 65: Brad Markel/Gamma-Liaison.
Page 90 © Bob Daemmrich//The Image Works, Inc.

Published by Julian Messner, a division of
Silver Burdett Press, Inc., Simon & Schuster, Inc.
Prentice Hall Bldg., Englewood Cliffs, NJ 07632

JULIAN MESSNER and colophon are trademarks of
Simon & Schuster, Inc. Design by Claire Counihan
Manufactured in the United States of America.

Lib. ed. 10 9 8 7 6 5 4 3 2 1

Library of Congress Cataloging-in-Publication Data
Kronenwetter, Michael.
Drugs in America / by Michael Kronenwetter.
p.   cm. — (Issues for the 90s)
Includes bibliographical references (p. 111)
Includes index.
Summary: Examines multiple aspects of America's drug problem, including the
variety of drugs available, the nature of drug abuse, the international drug trade, the
effects on society, and what is being done to improve the situation.
1. Drug abuse—United States—Juvenile literature.   2. Drug traffic—United
States—Juvenile literaure.   3. Narcotics, Control of—United States—Juvenile
literature.   [1. Drug abuse.   2. Drug traffic.   3. Narcotics, Control of.]
I. Title.   II. Series.
HV5825.K76   1990
362.29'0973—dc20   90-6339
                                                        CIP
ISBN 0-671-70557-1 (lib. bdg.)   AC

For Cathi and Jay

CONTENTS

CHAPTER ONE

BATTLEFRONTS

ON a Peruvian mountain slope, a tired peasant wipes his sweating brow. Ordinarily, the air is cool this high up, but today's sun is hotter than usual, and the peasant is tired. He lowers himself to the ground and stretches out among the shrublike coca plants that he is in the process of harvesting.

It feels good to lie down, but he knows he cannot rest too long. There is more work to do, and the sun is already past its high point in the sky. In only a few hours, it will reach the forested ridges in the west. Moments later, it will be too dark to work any more today.

Sunset comes quickly in the mountains.

The man reaches into his pocket and takes out a small pouch. It is filled with toasted leaves from these same coca plants. The leaves are mixed with wood ash. Taking some of this mixture between his fingers, he places it in his mouth. Slowly he begins to chew, pausing now and then to suck on a stick filled with lime. The lime stimulates the action of the coca leaves.

The chewing hurts him a little, because his gums are sensitive. The village where he has always lived is very small and isolated. He has never visited a dentist. The few teeth still left in his mouth are rotting.

Soon the man begins to feel better: stronger, ready to get on with his work. The brief rest and the dried coca leaves have done their job.

Eventually, the coca leaves that he is harvesting will be transformed into crack cocaine and sold on the streets of American cities.

A distinguished-looking man walks into a bank in Sydney, Australia. He asks to see the manager. Ushered into the manager's office, he explains that he plans to make a deposit of 100,000 Australian dollars—in cash. Later on, he says, he will want to make more large cash deposits and withdrawals. But, he emphasizes, the transactions must be carried out in ways that will not attract the attention of law-enforcement authorities. Such attention, he explains, would be "inconvenient" for his business.

He doesn't mention what his business is. He doesn't have to, because he has used this bank before. Both he and the bank manager understand that the man is a heroin trafficker. The money will be used to arrange for shipments of the drug, arriving from Hong Kong, to be sent safely out of Australia and on to the addicts of the United States and Canada.

A young man walks into a Mercedes Benz car dealership in suburban Chicago. He is carrying a bulging briefcase. When the salesperson comes up to him, he asks her about a sleek gray automobile sitting in the showroom.

After she has described all the features of the fully equipped, top-of-the-line automobile, the visitor asks how much it costs.

The salesperson is new at the dealership, and she wonders if she is being teased. The young man is flashily dressed and wears

In Peru's Upper Huallaga Valley, a peasant farmer harvests coca leaves, the raw material of cocaine.

a heavy chain around his neck that looks as if it is made of real gold. But he appears to be no more than 20 years old, and the way he speaks shows no trace of an education beyond grade school. How could he possibly afford such a car? Mercedes Benzes are extremely expensive.

"Seventy-nine thousand dollars," she answers, "plus tax."

Saying it, she assumes that the price will put an end to the young man's interest. But instead he grins and opens his briefcase. He removes several bundles of ten and twenty dollar bills and offers to pay for the car then and there. There are more bundles left in the briefcase.

The salesperson is astonished. She has never before had a customer purchase a car without bargaining for a lower price— much less pay for it in cash. In fact, she has never seen so much money in one place before.

She checks with the manager of the dealership about the unusual transaction. He is not surprised. The young man is probably a drug dealer, he explains. They often deal in cash. But should the dealership be taking money from a drug dealer? she asks.

Why not? responds the manager. His money is good.

The residents of the rundown street in a suburb of Kansas City, Missouri, are frightened. Their neighborhood has always been poor, but up until now it has at least been peaceful and law-abiding. The mixture of whites, blacks, and a few Hispanics has always gotten along. But suddenly a small wooden house in the middle of what was once a quiet block has become a center of crime and violence.

It was just a few months ago that a gang of young Jamaicans appeared in the neighborhood and moved into the house. Within days they had turned it into a crackhouse—a place where people come to purchase, and use, the powerful form of cocaine known as crack.

Ever since then, a parade of young men and women—most of them white—has been filing into and out of the house. The crime rate in the neighborhood has soared. Many longtime residents have been beaten and robbed on the streets by addicts looking for money to buy crack. Burglaries have increased. There have been stabbings and even murders.

When residents call the police to complain, they are told there is little that can be done right now. Although it is obvious what is going on inside, no one has any proof. And besides, crackhouses just like this one are popping up all over the city, and the police are badly overworked already.

Three men huddle together for warmth in a basement room of an abandoned tenement building in Detroit. Although it is winter, and the old building is unheated, two of them have their jackets off and their sleeves pushed up. The third has a pants leg rolled up. Each is searching his scarred skin for a vein into which he can shoot the drug heroin, to which they are all addicted.

Between them, they have gathered just enough heroin to keep them all going another day. Even so, they have only one needle. They will share it. They have heard about the danger of catching AIDS and other deadly diseases from shared needles, but they are too desperate for their "fix" to care.

Behind the windowless back wall of a high school gymnasium in Madison, Wisconsin, five girls gather at lunchtime. Two of them compare notes on the algebra test they took in third period. The rest discuss the dance coming up on Friday night. One of them takes a joint of marijuana out of her purse and lights it. As they continue to talk, they pass the joint around.

A well-dressed man walks briskly down the hallway of the main courthouse in downtown Atlanta, Georgia. He is a lawyer and is just about to give the closing argument in an important case. He has been up all night preparing his summation, and he is feeling tired, tense, and a little frightened of the challenge ahead.

He enters a men's room and slips into an empty stall. He turns the lock of the door behind him. Getting down on all fours, he looks under the partitions that separate his stall from those on either side. Both are empty.

Feeling safe for the moment, he gets to his feet. He takes a tiny spoon and an envelope of powdered cocaine out of the inside pocket of his suit jacket. He raises a spoonful of the white powder to his nose and inhales quickly. The rush he feels inspires him with sudden confidence. From experience, he knows the feeling will not last long. But, with luck, he hopes it will last just long enough to get him through his summation.

In the neonatal ward of a major hospital in Seattle, Washington, a newborn baby is screaming in agony and terror. He is suffering the pains of withdrawal from heroin. His mother is a long-term addict. During his life in the womb, he became used to the heroin flowing through his veins in the blood he shared with his mother. He became, in effect, a heroin addict himself, even before he was born. But now he is producing his own blood supply and has lost his source of heroin. His little body is seized with painful spasms brought on by its intense craving for the drug.

This baby is lucky. The doctors are aware of his problem, and they will probably be able to nurse him safely through withdrawal. He has a good chance of growing up strong and healthy. Another baby, not far away in the same hospital, is not so lucky. She is HIV positive. That is, she is carrying the AIDS virus and will almost certainly come down with the incurable disease within a few years. Then she will die.

The baby got the virus from her mother, who is a crack user. Her mother got it when she was raped by an AIDS-infected addict in a crackhouse. At the time, she was too high on the drug to care what was happening to her.

The scenes described here are representative. Events like these are taking place every day. Many similar events will take place while you are reading this book. Each of them comes from a different battlefront in the same deadly war that is raging across America and around the world—the drug war.

The danger posed by illegal drugs has been recognized for at least three decades. President Richard Nixon declared the first so-called war on drugs in the early 1970s. But by the mid-1980s, there were many more drug addicts—and drug-related crimes—than ever before. President Ronald Reagan declared a second war on drugs in 1986. President George Bush declared a third in 1989.

But the real drug war is not the struggle these different administrations have waged against drugs. The real drug war is the war that drugs—and the people who trade in them—are waging against American society.

Drugs destroy individual lives. But they do much, much more than that. They damage public health. They multiply the rate of crime. They corrupt police and other public officials. They build fear, hostility, and distrust between the races. They drain America's economic resources, and they distract attention from the many other serious problems that cry out to be solved.

Despite all the "wars on drugs," many millions of lives and many billions of dollars are still being sacrificed to the demand for illegal drugs. Polls show that large numbers of people consider drugs the country's worst problem. Measuring the threats that might face them in the 1990s, they are more frightened of drugs than of attack by a foreign power. More frightened of drugs than of terrorism. More frightened of drugs than of economic collapse and depression.

Their leaders feel the same. "All of us agree," declares President George Bush, "that the gravest domestic threat facing our nation today is drugs." Others, like Representatives Bill Alexander of Arkansas and Jamie Whitten of Mississippi, go even further. They call drugs the single most serious threat to the nation's security, either foreign or domestic.

Only a few other voices, like those of Eric Sterling, the president of the Criminal Justice Policy Foundation, warn that the fear of drugs might be overdone. Although drugs are a serious problem, they are just one of many terrible problems facing the country. By focusing so much attention on drugs, these voices warn, we could be in danger of ignoring even more desperate problems—like poverty, racism, and other forms of injustice.

In this book, we will investigate the many fronts of the drug war. We will explore the reasons people use illicit drugs. We will investigate the massive international trade in them. We will add up the enormous economic, social, and moral price society pays for them. And finally, we will examine the efforts our government is making to combat drugs, and the chances that those efforts will be successful.

CHAPTER TWO

APPEALING

POISONS

"**D**RUG**"** is not a precise term. In a broad sense, a drug is any substance that can be used as a medicine, or as an ingredient in a medicine. Drugs can be swallowed, injected, inhaled, or even absorbed through the skin. The changes they produce can be physical, mental, emotional, or all of these things at once.

Some drugs are extremely dangerous. Others are considered to be relatively safe.

Many drugs are useful in fighting disease. The antibiotics doctors prescribe to kill harmful germs are drugs. The epinephrine people with asthma inhale to help open up their lungs so they can breathe is a drug. Even aspirin is a drug. In fact, *all* medicines are drugs.

But so are many nonmedical substances, like the nicotine in cigarettes, the alcohol in beer and liquor, and the caffeine in coffee and cola drinks. And so are a variety of illegal substances, like heroin, marijuana, and cocaine.

In this book, the word "drug" will be used to mean any substance that is taken into the body to produce a chemical change in the user's condition. But we will be most concerned with those illegal substances that are used primarily to alter the mind or mood of the person who takes them.

ABUSING DRUGS

The illicit drugs we will talk about in this book are poisons. They can—and sometimes do—cause illness and death to the people who misuse them. What is more, the damage they do extends far beyond the individuals who take them. As we will see, these poisons seep into the veins and tissues of our whole society.

But these drugs are appealing and seductive poisons. They have immediate effects that are pleasant and seem desirable to the people who take them. It is these effects that lure the people who use drugs into poisoning themselves, and society along with them. These effects are sometimes described as "mind altering," or "mood altering."

The misuse of dangerous drugs is commonly referred to as "drug abuse." This is a misleading term, because it is not really drugs that are being abused, but the person who takes them. It is his or her body that is polluted by the drug. It is his or her mind that is twisted—and sometimes destroyed.

The distinction between using and abusing an illegal drug is a controversial one. Not everyone makes this kind of distinction. For a small minority, who don't believe in drugs of any kind, using even a legal drug is a form of drug abuse. For others, only the use of an illegal drug should be classified as abuse. For still others, the distinction is not a matter of *which* drug is used, but *how much* of it. They find the moderate use of any drug, legal or illegal, to be acceptable so long as it doesn't interfere with the rights or safety of others. And, in a few people's eyes, virtually anything goes. For them, the only real form of drug abuse is a fatal overdose.

In this book, when we talk about drug abuse, we mean any nonmedical use of a drug that may cause serious harm—to the user or to anyone else. By this definition, some drugs might be used without abusing them./ One or two drinks of alcohol, for example, are not a serious risk for a healthy adult. A few tablespoons of cough medicine containing the drug codeine are not likely to cause harm either. But even these relatively harmless drugs can be extremely dangerous when taken in large amounts or over a long period of time.

In fact, virtually any drug can be abused. Too much of almost any substance can be harmful. People have been known to overdose on aspirin. Sometimes the difference between using a drug and abusing it depends on the circumstances. Some drugs only become dangerous when taken along with other drugs. Certain kinds of very helpful medicines can become extremely dangerous, even life-threatening, when taken along with alcohol, for example.

On the other hand, some drugs cannot be used at all without abusing them. Their effects are so powerful, or so unpredictable, that they cannot be taken safely. Crack cocaine, for example, has been known to kill people the first time they used it—even when they took it in amounts that caused other people no physical harm at all.

DRUG ADDICTION

Some users get "hooked." That is, they become addicted to their drug. They become dependent on it. There are two basic kinds of drug addiction: physical dependence and psychological dependence. (Some experts do not like to use "dependence" and "addiction" as synonyms. They argue that there is a technical difference. But that difference is not important to this discussion.)

People who are *physically* dependent on a drug cannot stop

using it without suffering physical symptoms known as withdrawal. Typical symptoms of drug withdrawal are nausea, diarrhea, cramps, and various kinds of pain. The nature and seriousness of these symptoms vary with different drugs. They also depend on the extent of the individual's addiction. In some cases, withdrawal symptoms are relatively mild. In others, they are severe enough to kill.

Ironically, people who become addicted to a drug tend to develop a tolerance for it. That is, they begin to need more and more of it. If they start out needing one pill to make them feel high, they later find they need two—then three—then a handful. Finally, in some cases, it becomes impossible for them to achieve whatever sensation they began taking the drug for in the first place. But they end up taking more and more of it anyway, just in order to avoid suffering the agony of withdrawal.

Not all drugs are physically addicting in this way. But almost any drug can be psychologically addicting. People who are *psychologically* dependent on a drug come to need it in order to feel at ease, or satisfied. Without it, they feel deprived. They become anxious, depressed, and irritable. They may even become irrational. Even though psychological addicts may not suffer any physical withdrawal symptoms, they still find it hard—and sometimes impossible—to stop taking the drug.

Although physical and psychological dependence are two different things, each is a very real and very serious addiction. It is possible to be *both* psychologically and physically addicted to the same drug. It is also possible to be addicted to more than one drug at the same time.

Many drug addicts suffer through repeated bouts of heavy drug use during much of their lives. They can never be sure that they have finally shaken free of drugs once and for all. The popular country and western singer Johnny Cash has wrestled with drugs for 35 years. In a recent television interview, he vividly expressed the haunting nature of drug abuse. "I hate mood altering drugs," he declared. "I hate everything about mood altering drugs. I hate what they've done to me [and] I don't plan to use them again. But I might."

CATEGORIES OF DRUGS

People use and abuse drugs for many reasons. They take them for recreation and for pleasure. They use them to lift their confidence, to improve their mood, or to change the way they view reality. They use them to relieve their pains, both physical and emotional. They use them to relax. They use them to give them energy when they are tired and to put them to sleep when they are not. They even use them to alter, or do away with, the effects of other drugs.

Most of the drugs that people abuse fall into one of the following categories:

Narcotics include drugs such as opium, morphine, codeine, and heroin. These four drugs are sometimes called opiates, because they are all made from a plant called the opium poppy. Chemically manufactured narcotics, such as methadone and meperidine, are called opioids.

Medically, narcotics like morphine are used primarily to lessen the feeling of pain. They do this in two ways. First, they have an anesthetic effect, reducing the awareness of pain. Second, they change the way a person reacts to pain. Narcotics also tend to reduce the sex drive, and they sometimes have undesirable psychological side effects as well.

Narcotics give people a feeling of euphoria, an exaggerated sense of well-being. No matter what is actually happening to the user, he or she tends to feel at peace and satisfied with it. It is this feeling, more than the anesthetic effect, that leads people to abuse narcotics. Ultimately, for those who get hooked, it becomes impossible to feel really comfortable without them. Overdoses sometimes result when addicts need ever greater amounts of narcotics to achieve the same feeling of euphoria. Death from narcotics overdose generally results from the failure of the respiratory (breathing) system.

Narcotics such as heroin and morphine are taken by injection. For this reason, these drugs tend to be associated with the spread of AIDS, hepatitis, and other serious infections.

Stimulants are drugs that excite (or stimulate) the body's central nervous system. They include the so-called uppers, such as cocaine, and the amphetamines, such as methamphetamine. They also include some inhalants, such as certain airplane glues, aerosols, and nail polishes. Although these substances are not manufactured as drugs, some people use them to stimulate themselves. As with other categories of drugs, the strength and effects of different stimulants vary widely.

Doctors sometimes prescribe stimulants to relieve tiredness or to increase the energy of sluggish patients. Drug abusers, however, usually take them to produce "highs" or "rushes"— feelings of sudden and intense pleasure. Once the drug wears off, abusers often experience "lows." These can range from mild feelings of exhaustion to insomnia, and from a general sense of sadness to severe depression.

Strong stimulants are physically dangerous. They can cause such symptoms as an abnormally rapid heart beat, convulsions, and stomach disorders. In large doses (or acting on people who have physical problems to begin with) they can bring on heart attacks and death. Over the long term, some stimulants can cause permanent heart and lung damage. They can also cause psychoses—serious mental disorders that distort a person's sense of reality and ability to cope with life. These disorders include paranoia, an intense and unreasoning sense of fear and suspicion, as well as conditions similar to the mental disease of schizophrenia.

Depressants, or *sedatives,* are the opposite of stimulants. Sometimes called "downers," they depress the central nervous system. This has a soothing, or calming, effect on the user. For this reason, they are often prescribed as tranquilizers or sleeping aids. The sedatives most often medically prescribed are barbiturates such as Nembutal and Seconal and tranquilizers such as Valium and Librium. But by far the most frequently used of all the depressants is alcohol.

Sometimes depressants can be *too* soothing. They can lead to forgetfulness and confusion. This can cause users to lose track of how much of the drug they've already taken. For this reason, accidental overdoses of depressants tend to be even more common than overdoses of most other drugs.

Among the short-term effects of abusing depressants are tiredness, nausea, constipation, blurred vision and speech, and an inability to function sexually. Long-term misuse of depressants can lead to brain and liver damage.

Hallucinogens, or *psychedelics,* change the way the user experiences the outside world. They alter the way he or she sees, hears, and smells. They can also affect the user's mood and cause drastic changes in his or her thought processes.

Hallucinogens sometimes produce states very similar to certain mental illnesses in which reality is distorted. Those who take them sometimes hear voices. Some users see strange— occasionally beautiful, occasionally terrifying—visions. Some have the sense that sights are heard or that sounds are seen.

Because these experiences can seem like visits to another place, another dimension of reality, they are sometimes called "trips." A "good trip" is one that produces pleasant experiences or what appear to be new insights. A "bad trip" is one that produces terror or dangerously irrational behavior. People on bad trips have been known to become violent or to leap from high windows, believing they can fly.

Some hallucinogens, such as mescaline, which is made from the peyote cactus, are natural substances. Others, such as LSD (lysergic acid diethylamide) and PCP (phencyclidine), are synthetically produced from chemicals in a laboratory.

Cannabis, or *hemp,* is a plant from which a number of drugs are produced. In the United States, the most common variety of cannabis is marijuana. Other forms of cannabis are ganja, which is grown in Jamaica, and bhang, which comes from India.

The most often used part of the cannabis plant is the leaf, which is dried and smoked in cigarettes or pipes, like tobacco. "Pot," as it is called, can also be chewed or added as an ingredient to foods. Hashish, or "hash," is a more powerful drug, made from the resins of the cannabis plant.

Cannabis can make some users so relaxed that they fall asleep.

Others become intensely excited or amused. Many users report that their physical senses are greatly heightened. Smells smell stronger, sounds sound clearer, and colors look brighter. But some users have hallucinations. Others become anxious, or even panic-stricken. Some become argumentative, and sometimes hostile.

There is reason to fear that the physical effects of smoking cannabis leaf may be similar to those of smoking tobacco. There have also been reports that heavy pot-smoking can lead to brain damage.

THE LEGAL DRUGS

This book will deal mostly with illegal drugs. They are the ones that receive the most attention. They are the ones that support the vast criminal empires that run the international drug trade. And they are the ones that three recent American presidents have declared war against. But they are not the only drugs that threaten the well-being of our society.

A drug doesn't have to be illegal for people to abuse it—or to become addicted to it. More Americans are probably addicted to alcohol, a legal drug, than to all the illegal drugs put together. It is not unusual for patients to abuse tranquilizers prescribed for them by their doctors. Nor is it unusual for people to become psychologically addicted to codeine, cough medicines, or other drugs sold over the counter.

Legal drugs can be just as harmful as illegal ones. Some are even more harmful than some of the drugs that are outlawed. Alcohol is probably the leading example of a drug that is both legal and dangerous. A depressant, alcohol is a major cause of cirrhosis of the liver and other fatal diseases. It is also a factor in about half of all traffic deaths.

Nicotine and other substances found in tobacco contribute to all three of the leading killer diseases—heart disease, cancer, and stroke. They also play an important part in emphysema, bronchitis, and birth defects, as well as several other diseases. In

1985 the then U.S. surgeon general, C. Everett Koop, announced that smoking had caused 390,000 deaths in the United States in that year alone. That was far more than all the deaths caused by illegal drugs in any given decade.

Even a seemingly harmless drug like caffeine, which young children drink in soft drinks, has side effects. It is a stimulant that can cause nervousness, tension, and irritability in some people. Physically, it constricts (or narrows) the blood vessels. Large doses of caffeine can be dangerous to people whose circulation is already poor because of disease. It can even increase the risk of frostbite in the fingers and toes of a healthy person in extremely cold weather.

THE REAL RISKS OF USING DRUGS

In the 1950s it was widely believed that even one marijuana cigarette could lead straight to heroin addiction. In the 1960s many young people believed there was no risk at all in using marijuana, and very little risk in using harder drugs.

Today we know that the risks of using some kinds of drugs are not as extreme as people once thought. But we also know that there are real risks involved in experimenting with any drug. Unfortunately, we do not know exactly how great the risks will be for any particular drug user.

The most serious immediate risk in using drugs is the risk of death—either from an overdose or from some kind of allergic reaction. People have died from using cocaine just once. Their hearts suddenly stopped. This risk is very low with a drug like marijuana, but it can be quite high with a drug like crack cocaine or the new amphetamine, "ice."

But death from overdose is not the only immediate danger from using drugs. There are also the potential dangers associated with any kind of intoxication. Many illegal drugs alter both perceptions and behavior. This can lead to accidents. Driving a car under the influence of marijuana or LSD can be every bit as dangerous as driving under the influence of alcohol. Drugs can

Drug abusers sometimes "snort" cocaine through a thin straw.

also lead people to do things they would otherwise not have done. Stimulants and hallucinogens have led normally peaceful people to commit acts of violence, for example. Opiates have led many others into dangerous sexual behavior.

There are also medical risks involved in the long-term use of any drug, whether that drug is legal or not. The risks can be particularly great with illegal drugs. That is because specific batches of illegal drugs are not tested for purity or quality, and the use of such drugs is not supervised by a physician or other medical expert.)

But the most important risk for potential drug users is the danger of becoming addicted. The fact is that anyone may or may not become psychologically addicted to almost any drug, and not just to so-called recreational drugs.

There is no way to tell in advance whether addiction will happen to you. The odds vary from drug to drug and from user to user. There is little concrete statistical evidence concerning the addictive power of most drugs, but the evidence for some is better than for others.

(For example, it is generally accepted that the risk of becoming addicted to alcohol is about 15 percent. That is, about 15 out of every 100 people who experiment with alcohol will become addicted at some time in their lives. But the risk of addiction to illegal drugs is much more controversial. Because using them is against the law, people tend to conceal the fact that they use them. This makes it difficult to get reliable figures.

Some experts believe the risk of becoming addicted to marijuana is about the same as the risk with alcohol. Others say it is higher. Some argue that the risk is increasing as the marijuana in use becomes stronger and stronger in its effects.

The risks involved in using physically addicting drugs such as heroin and cocaine may be even higher. According to the National Institute on Drug Abuse, about 1 out of every 10 people (or 10 percent) who have used cocaine at all in the past year are frequent users now. The actual risk of becoming addicted to cocaine is probably higher than 10 percent, however. Many of today's casual users will undoubtedly become addicted in the future. Some estimates of the odds range as high as 1 in 6—the same odds you would have playing Russian roulette with a six-shot revolver.

Crack cocaine is probably the most addictive of today's most widely used drugs. Estimates of the percentage of crack users who get hooked range as high as 85 percent—or more than 8 in 10! As the former surgeon general of the United States, C. Everett Koop, has said, "I don't know of any way a person can take crack over any period of time without the risk of addiction."

A survey of medical examiners reported that in 1988 3,308 deaths were caused by cocaine or crack, and another 2,480 by heroin. (Marijuana deaths weren't included in the survey. But there were undoubtedly far fewer of those. (One estimate for marijuana deaths is only 75 per year.) But the survey was incomplete. It only covered 27 cities. Even in those, several deaths from drugs probably went misdiagnosed or unreported.

There is no way to predict who will, and who will not, have problems with drugs. Certainly fame and money are no protection. The list of famous and successful people who have wrestled with drugs seems endless. It includes singers like Johnny Cash; popular performers like Liza Minelli, Richard Pryor, and Ben Vereen; rock stars like ex-Beatle Ringo Starr, Belinda Carlisle, and Eric Clapton; football players like Dexter Manley, the Washington Redskins defensive star who was banned from the National Football League for life because of repeated drug use, and Mercury Morris, who went to prison because of his association with drugs; as well as basketball stars like John Lucas of the Houston Rockets.

Many prominent people have died from drugs. Among the most famous are the 1960s comedian and satirist Lenny Bruce; the legendary rock singers Janis Joplin and Jim Morrison; the one-time heavyweight boxing champion Sonny Liston; and one of the original stars of *Saturday Night Live,* John Belushi.

The dangers of cocaine were first brought home to many young Americans in 1986, when the college basketball superstar Len Bias died from using cocaine. The 22-year-old had snorted the drug while celebrating the brilliant future he expected as the first draft choice of the NBA champion Boston Celtics team.

Several children of famous people have also fallen victim to drugs. They include a son of former Attorney General Robert Kennedy (and nephew of President John F. Kennedy); a son of the Academy Award-winning actor Paul Newman; and a son of Bart Starr, the Green Bay Packer quarterback who was the Most Valuable Player in the first two Super Bowls.

While many people suffer greatly from using drugs, many others do not. Some people use drugs once or twice, or even casually over a period of time, and never have any serious problems as a result. This fact lures many young people into experimenting with drugs. Because some people use drugs without suffering obvious consequences, they decide the odds are on their side. Why not give drugs a try?

In reality, the statistical odds don't mean very much to a particular individual who experiments with a dangerous drug. What matters is what will happen to that person. Will he or she, personally, get into trouble with drugs?

And the answer to that question is completely—and terrifyingly—unpredictable.

CHAPTER THREE

A SHORT HISTORY
OF DRUG ABUSE

DRUG use is nothing new. People have been using and abusing drugs for thousands of years. For most of that time, and in most places, alcohol has been the most widely abused of all drugs. But it has rarely been alone. The opium poppy, for instance, was grown by the Sumerians at least 6,000 years ago, and by the Greeks and the Romans after that.

Cannabis has been in use in parts of Asia for at least 5,000 years. There is evidence that the Scythians burned cannabis seeds as incense in their religious ceremonies 2,500 years ago. In the eleventh century a terrorist cult from Persia, whose members were known for committing vicious murders, was called the Hashish-ans. The Europeans, who feared them, believed they took hashish to work themselves up to their bloody acts. It is from "Hashish-an" that we get the word *assassin*.

Scores of different mushrooms and other psychedelic plants

were used by ancient cultures from the Middle East to the Western Hemisphere. By the time Columbus arrived in the New World in the fifteenth century, the inhabitants had already been chewing, smoking, drinking, and sniffing various forms of drugs for many centuries.

Among these was coca, which is the raw material for cocaine. The Spanish colonizers of Peru noticed that chewing coca leaves caused the native Incas to lose their appetites, and at the same time gave them energy. From that time on, the Spaniards used coca to take advantage of the Incas, forcing them to work in their gold and silver mines. By giving them coca, the Spaniards made sure that the Incas would have plenty of energy for work, while needing practically no food to keep them going.

Opium began to be a serious problem in China in the seventeenth and eighteenth centuries. It was imported into that country from India, where the opium poppy grew most abundantly. Eventually, the number of Chinese opium addicts rose into the millions. From the late 1700s on, the Chinese government launched efforts to discourage its citizens from smoking what they called the "foreign mud."

But the English had built up a very profitable trade, shipping opium from their Indian colony to China. American ships also played a part in this trade. Among the Americans who got rich by trading in opium was Warren Delano, who would become the grandfather of President Franklin Delano Roosevelt.

When China tried to stop this trade, the British went to war to keep it going. They won the so-called Opium Wars of 1839 and 1858 and forced the Chinese to let the opium trade continue. The Chinese government then followed the ancient American proverb, "If you can't lick 'em, join 'em," by making it legal for Chinese farmers to grow opium poppies. By 1900 there were around 15 million opium addicts in China.

Although the British ended the legal opium trade early in the twentieth century, other effects of the Opium Wars remained. For one thing, the island of Hong Kong became a long-term colony of Britain, which it still is today. (It is scheduled to be returned to China in 1997.) And opium addiction continued to be an enormous problem in China until the Communist government clamped down on it in 1949.

DRUGS IN THE UNITED STATES

The custom of smoking opium came to America with Chinese immigrants in the nineteenth century. They came to lay track for the railroads that were then being built to link the industrial centers of the East with the farmlands of the Middle West and the Pacific Coast.

Morphine, which is made from opium, became a serious problem for soldiers during the Civil War. Used to kill the pain of those wounded in battle, it was more effective than opium because it could be injected directly into the bloodstream. Unfortunately, it was also more addictive. Many soldiers left both the Union and Confederate armies addicted to morphine.

Heroin, an opiate made from morphine, was introduced in 1898. At first it was added to cough medicines, because it deadened the impulse to cough. (Codeine, which is also made from morphine, is still used in some cough medicines today.) At first, many scientists and doctors assumed that heroin wasn't addicting. They even hoped that it would provide the answer to morphine addiction. But the doctors were wrong. If anything, heroin was even more physically addictive than morphine. It was also more powerful.

Most of the early heroin abusers were women. Some of them first became addicted to morphine given to them by doctors to help them through childbirth. The same doctors then prescribed heroin to help them counter their morphine addiction.

Heroin produced an intense high that lured many people into taking it for reasons that had nothing to do with medicine. In the early twentieth century, pharmacists may have been surprised at how many customers who showed no sign of a cold came into their stores to buy cough medicine.

By the 1920s people were beginning to inject heroin, like morphine, directly into their bloodstreams. It wasn't long before heroin addiction was a more serious problem in the United States than morphine addiction had ever been.

The manufacture of heroin was banned in the United States in 1924. It was no longer legal for any purpose, medical or otherwise. The medicinal use of morphine continued, however, and many doctors continue to use it today. It is still one of the most effective painkillers available.

Although since the Civil War doctors have done their best to avoid addicting their patients to morphine, this has not always been possible, particularly in wartime. World Wars I and II and the Korean War each contributed a new batch of morphine addicts to American society.

In the late nineteenth century, cocaine (or cocaine hydrochloride) became the new drug of choice for many people in both Europe and America. It was most commonly taken in the form of a white powder. This was snorted, or inhaled, through the nose. It could also be eaten or dissolved in a solution and injected into the user's veins. The latter method produced the most powerful effects.

Cocaine gave its users a rush of energy. It also made them feel alert and clearheaded, as if their mind had been suddenly sharpened. For this reason, it was popular among some intellectuals. One of them was the great pioneer of psychiatry, Dr. Sigmund Freud. Not only did he experiment with cocaine himself, but he prescribed it for others until the drug drove one of his patients mad.

But the best-known nineteenth-century user of cocaine was a fictional character named Sherlock Holmes. When Sir Arthur Conan Doyle created this brilliant detective in 1887, he made him a cocaine user. Holmes would inject himself with cocaine three times a day for months at a time. He used it, Holmes told his friend Dr. John Watson, because it was so "stimulating and clarifying to the mind."

But Doyle, who was a doctor himself, knew the harm that cocaine could do. And so he had his fictional Dr. Watson warn Holmes to "Count the cost! Your brain may, as you say, be roused and excited, but it is a pathological and morbid process which...may leave a permanent weakness. You know, too, what a black reaction comes upon you. Surely the game is hardly worth the candle. Why should you, for a mere passing pleasure, risk the loss of those great powers with which you have been endowed?" Like many real-life drug abusers, however, Holmes refused to listen.

Like the opiates, cocaine was easily available in the early twentieth century. It could be bought without a prescription from pharmacies, and it was also used in a number of popular patent medicines. It was even added to wines—one of which received a hearty recommendation from both an American president and a pope!

Cocaine was also easily available to children, in the form of the soft drink Coca-Cola. In fact, Coca-Cola was named after the coca plant, from which cocaine is derived. Cocaine was removed from Coca-Cola, and from all other nonprescription products, in the early twentieth century. Even so, it remained readily available in several states.

In the early 1900s, most pharmacies had soda fountains, and as Senator Joseph Biden of Delaware explained at a Senate hearing, "All you had to do was sit down and order a soft drink. For a little extra, a gram of pure cocaine would be sprinkled into it—legally." The easy availability of cocaine led to what Biden has called the first "great epidemic" of drug abuse in U.S. history.

In 1924 the government banned all nonmedical uses of cocaine, as well as of most narcotics. Outlawing them did not get rid of them, however. Many people continued to use the drugs, and some abused them heavily. But, for the next several decades, at least, illegal drug abuse was limited to certain groups in society—and usually to a small minority within those groups.

Morphine addiction was largely confined to ex-soldiers and others who had been given morphine after long-term painful injuries. Heroin addiction was primarily limited to some of the nation's racial minorities, particularly in the ghettos (the segregated black and Hispanic neighborhoods) of certain big cities.

Cocaine use was even more limited, although to a very

different segment of society. Only some of the most daring members of the wealthier classes were cocaine users, together with a handful of jazz musicians.

Marijuana was also used by jazz musicians, perhaps even more widely than cocaine. Marijuana became associated with other people in show business as well. But it was also used by ordinary people living in the West and Midwest, where it grew wild.

In the 1950s, doctors began prescribing larger and larger quantities of barbiturates and stimulants for their patients. Most of the people who took them were respectable, middle-class citizens who thought of themselves as law-abiding. But some fell into the habit of abusing the drugs. Eventually, many began seeing several different doctors, in order to get several prescriptions at once.

A black market sprang up, centered mostly around college campuses, where more and more students began "popping" pills for "kicks." By the 1960s about eight times as many barbiturates were being manufactured as in the 1940s. About half of them were making their way into the black market. At the same time, heroin use was also on the rise.

DRUG USE IN THE '60s

From the time most recreational drugs were outlawed in the 1920s, until the 1960s, the number of illegal drug users went up and down. But it always remained relatively small. The number of real addicts and other serious drug abusers remained even smaller. Even marijuana, which was the most widely used of all the illegal drugs, wasn't considered a major social problem. There simply were not enough users to get all worked up about.

But in the 1960s drug use soared. What is more, drugs began to spread throughout all levels of society. For the first time, illegal drugs were taken up by large numbers of people from virtually every economic, social, and racial group in the country. Most of these legions of new drug users were young.

For many young people the 1960s was a time of anger and rebellion. In that decade, young Americans took a hard look at some grim realities. One was the system of racial segregation that still shut black people out of many parts of American society a hundred years after the Civil War. Another was the poverty that still crushed millions of Americans, white and black, in the richest country on Earth. And still another was the war in Vietnam, which many young people did not understand and many others considered to be morally wrong.

Some of these young people reacted with undirected hostility and rebellion. Others turned their anger to political protest. Hundreds of thousands of young people took to the streets in massive political demonstrations. Some publicly burned their draft cards, even though doing so was illegal. Some went to work to help the poor, to register black voters in the South, or to support politicians who opposed the war.

Significant numbers of people in each of these groups took drugs. For many, drugs became a kind of political symbol—a challenge to a society they considered to be corrupt and hypocritical.

For some, drugs became more than a symbol of rebellion. They became the focus of a whole life-style. A one-time Harvard psychology professor, Dr. Timothy Leary, called on young people to "turn on" to psychedelic drugs, to "tune in" to the visions they produced, and to "drop out" of mainstream American society. Many did. Calling themselves "hippies," they set out to invent a new way of living—one they pledged would be free of the greed they felt was at the heart of American society.

For the hippies, drugs became the key to a new way of thinking about life and the world around them. Like Timothy Leary, they believed that drugs—particularly marijuana and LSD—were "mind-expanding." They considered the "trips" they took on these drugs to be voyages into new realms of understanding.

Meanwhile, a very different crop of new drug users was being produced by the war in Vietnam. Cannabis and heroin were

American soldiers in Vietnam in the early 1970s found it easy to get heroin—and to get addicted.

plentiful in and around the military bases there. Escape into drugs was a great temptation for American military personnel, tired and sickened by the horrible realities of war.

There is no way to tell how many American heroin addicts the war in Vietnam produced. But as many as half the members of some American military units reportedly used the drug occasionally. Use was so high in the early 1970s that it is estimated that as many as 20 percent of the Americans who were in Vietnam at that time were at least temporarily addicted. Thousands of them brought their addictions home. Many thousands more came home accustomed to using drugs.

THE CHANGING ATTITUDE TOWARD DRUGS

Protesters, hippies, and soldiers were not the only ones turning to drugs in the 1960s and '70s. They led the way, but many other young Americans followed. Drugs were flowing throughout the culture in those years, like rain running down a windowpane. Popular television shows—particularly the ones watched by young people, shows like *Laugh-In* and *The Smothers Brothers*—made drugs the subject of jokes. People who seriously objected to drug use were made the butt of such jokes. They were portrayed as old-fashioned, naive, and "decidedly uncool." Some of the most popular rock groups of the era, including the Beatles, sang songs that seemed to be based on psychedelic drug trips.

Most of the new drug users of the 1960s were of college age, or slightly older. Few of them worried that they might be doing serious harm to themselves. After all, they felt, their elders had misled them about other things—they were probably wrong about the bad effects of drugs as well.

To some extent, this was true. In the 1950s and early '60s, a lot of misinformation about drugs was being passed down from adults to young people. Most parents knew very little about drugs. They had never used them themselves, and they didn't know anyone else who had. All they really knew was that drugs were dangerous and illegal. That was more than enough reason to fear what they could do to their children. Acting out of their own fears, they tried to frighten their children away from drugs. In their efforts, unfortunately, they often showed their own ignorance of the reality of drug abuse.

To hear many adults tell it, a single marijuana cigarette would be the first step on the pathway to certain doom. Marijuana, they told their children, would inevitably lead to LSD or to heroin addiction, to madness, and finally to death.

As drug use of all kinds became more common during the

1960s, it became clearer and clearer that this just wasn't true. Many young people knew someone who had used marijuana, or even LSD. These casual users may have acted strangely when they were high on drugs, but they weren't going crazy. And most of them weren't turning to harder drugs either. That was fortunate, because by 1972, a presidential commission estimated that 24 million Americans had already tried marijuana at least once!

Most young people who got close to the "drug scene" at all saw a friend on a bad "trip" on LSD or some other drug. They may even have known people who overdosed on one drug or another. But such events seemed to be rare exceptions. Most of the drug users they knew or heard about seemed to show few bad effects from taking drugs.

So, many young people reasoned, if marijuana didn't lead to madness, maybe there was nothing wrong with it at all. And, if there was nothing wrong with marijuana, maybe there was nothing wrong with heroin either. Or LSD. Or cocaine.

In short, many young people began to doubt everything adults had ever told them about drugs. (Particularly since some of these adults were sipping martinis or swallowing tranquilizers at the time.) And, although actual use of illegal drugs was largely confined to people of college age or older, this distrust began to spread among people of high school age as well.

Most young people—even those of college age—never seriously abused drugs in the 1960s and early '70s. Many of them never used any hard drugs at all. Even so, the period saw a sudden and dramatic shift in the American attitude toward illegal drugs.

Before the 1960s most Americans, young and old, had been frightened and appalled by the idea of using illegal drugs. They regarded drugs not only as dangerous but as shameful. Drug users were looked upon as disreputable, and either pathetic or evil, depending on their social status. But in the 1960s, drug use became commonplace among the young. Even many of those who never used drugs themselves tolerated drug use by others.

The 1960s, then, marked a watershed in the history of illegal drugs in America. For the first time, many of America's young people began to take illicit drugs for granted—to accept them as a fact of life.

They have been a fact of life in America ever since.

CHAPTER FOUR

DRUGS

OF CHOICE

ACCORDING to the National Institute on Drug Abuse, 14.5 million Americans currently use illegal drugs. Between them, they use every kind of illegal drug already mentioned, and many others besides. In addition, new drugs are appearing all the time. But the vast majority of all illegal drug users still use one or more of the big three—marijuana, heroin, and cocaine.

MARIJUANA

Of the three, marijuana is the most widely used. About one out of every four Americans between the ages of 18 and 45 has used the drug at least once in the last year. A 1985 poll by the National Institute on Drug Abuse showed that about 18 million people has used it in the month the survey was taken. And altogether it is estimated that the U.S. marijuana market is worth about $16 billion every year.

Traditionally, cannabis has always been regarded a little differently from most other illegal drugs. In the 1960s and '70s, many parents who were opposed to illegal drugs in general were somewhat less concerned about marijuana than about the others. They worried less about marijuana itself than about what it might lead to. They warned against it as the first step on the road that could lead to stronger, more dangerous drugs.

And, in fact, in most of its forms it is weaker than the other, "harder" drugs. This is not to say that marijuana is not dangerous. It can cause hallucinations; even when it doesn't, it distorts perceptions of space and depth, disrupts the ability to think, impairs judgment, and greatly increases the chance of accidents. Nevertheless, its effects are less drastic than those of many other drugs.

What is more, unlike both heroin and crack, marijuana is now widely regarded as nonaddictive. Also unlike cocaine or crack, it rarely, if ever, provokes violent behavior. In fact, it usually has a mellowing effect.

It is not surprising, then, that marijuana is sometimes considered to be a kind of amateur's drug. Those who use harder drugs think of marijuana the way a heavy whiskey drinker thinks of beer, or the way a coffee drinker thinks of tea. Unlike heroin or cocaine, cannabis can be homegrown. In places as different as Wisconsin and California, Florida and Maine, marijuana plants can be grown in people's backyards. They can even be grown on apartment balconies or in little boxes on windowsills. Furthermore, no complicated technology is needed to convert the cannabis plant into a usable drug. Its leaves can simply be dried, then rolled into a cigarette paper and smoked.

Still, most of the cannabis products used in the United States come from abroad, the bulk of them from Mexico. That is because, until recently, foreign cannabis products—like hashish from the Middle East, "Thai sticks" and "Buddha sticks" from Asia, and "Acapulco gold" from Mexico—were more highly prized than American-grown products. So were several other

Marijuana, the most widely used illegal drug in the United States, is usually smoked in hand-rolled cigarettes.

varieties from Morocco, Colombia, Jamaica, and elsewhere. That is because the foreign products were usually both stronger and purer than the American.

But recently a new variety of marijuana has been developed that can be grown in the United States and that is even more potent than most foreign varieties. The main mind-altering ingredient of marijuana is a chemical called THC (tetrahydrocannabinol). This new variety of homegrown marijuana can have as much as three to five times as much THC in its leaves as some foreign strains.

The seeds for this new variety still come from abroad.

Surprisingly, though, they don't come from such long-established cannabis-growing areas as Mexico or Asia. They come from Holland. The country that has long been famous for providing the world's best tulip bulbs now provides some of the world's best cannabis seeds as well. And, just as surprisingly, Americans can buy the seeds by mail order.

Because of this development, the lure of foreign cannabis seems to wearing off. Today about 25 percent of the marijuana used in the United States is grown here. Some of it is grown by individuals for their own use. Some is grown by large-scale growers who distribute their product across the country.

Because large marijuana fields might be easily spotted by the police, growers have found imaginative ways to hide their plants. Some have moved indoors, growing their crops in greenhouses under grow-lights. Others have sown their seeds in isolated regions of American's national forests. They are actually growing their illegal drug on public lands, owned by the very government that has declared war on drugs.

HEROIN

About 25 percent of the nation's serious drug abusers are heroin addicts. Most of them are concentrated in big cities, such as Chicago, New York, and Detroit. The great majority of them are male.

The opium poppy is grown in several countries, including Mexico and the Soviet Union. But most of the really high quality opium—the kind that makes the best heroin—comes from two parts of the world.

The first is the so-called Golden Crescent that sweeps down from Turkey in the west, through Iran and Afghanistan, to Pakistan. The second is the Golden Triangle of Southeast Asia, where Laos, Thailand, and Burma all come together in the hills just south of China. One thing these two regions have in common is a large area of mountainous land where the climate is temperate and cool. Another is the fact that the governments there are not in full control of their own countrysides. From these two "golden" fountains flows most of the heroin that enters the United States.

In recent years the popularity of heroin has grown rapidly, even while the popularity of some of the other illegal drugs has dropped. Not long ago the government estimated that there were fewer than 500,000 heroin addicts in the United States. Today, according to Agent Robert Stutman of the federal DEA (Drug Enforcement Administration), there are probably 250,000 heroin addicts in New York City alone. The Justice Department estimates that there are 750,000 addicts in the country as a whole, while other observers suspect that the real total may be even higher.

One reason for the old drug's new popularity involves a change in how it is used. In the past, American heroin users took heroin almost exclusively by needle. That fact alone kept many people from experimenting with it.

Needles are unpleasant to use at best. They leave telltale scars, called "tracks." And, worst of all, needles can spread deadly infections, such as hepatitis and the most dreaded of all modern diseases, AIDS. But in recent years, abusers have found ways of smoking heroin instead of injecting it. This method makes it easier to get involved with the drug in the first place. It also eliminates the danger of getting AIDS from a contaminated needle.

Another reason for the rising popularity of heroin may be the drop in price. According to figures quoted by *U.S. News & World Report,* world opium production soared about 50 percent between 1985 and 1989. Mostly as a result of this rapid rise in supply, prices on the street dropped at least 20 percent. And agricultural experts are predicting record opium crops for the early 1990s.

COCAINE

And yet, according to most drug-abuse experts, the biggest problem drug in America is neither marijuana nor heroin. It is cocaine. According to the National Institute on Drug Abuse figures quoted in Senate hearings, about eight million Americans used some form of cocaine in 1989. In 1990 about one million of them were using it at least once a week.

Cocaine is an incredibly profitable commodity. Of all the billions of dollars Americans spend on drugs each year, almost half goes to buy cocaine and crack. One indication of just how big the U.S. cocaine market really is came to light on September 29, 1989. On that day law officers raided a warehouse about 20 miles northwest of Los Angeles. Inside they found several truckloads of cocaine, all wrapped in neat parcels and packed in cardboard boxes. It added up to roughly 19 tons of the illegal white powder. The DEA reported that the cocaine in that one warehouse could have been sold to dealers for about $2 billion. Once those dealers had cut it, or converted it to crack, they could have sold it on the street for as much as $20 billion!

In the next few weeks, from October 1 to November 10, 1989, U.S. officials seized 45 more tons of cocaine in other actions. And yet, according to Robert Stutman, these immense seizures made little dent in the country's cocaine supply.

Up until the 1980s, almost all the cocaine used in the United States was snorted. In the '80s, however, more and more abusers turned to freebasing the drug. Freebasing is a fairly complicated and dangerous process. It involves exposing cocaine powder to ether and transforming it into smokable crystals. These crystals produce a much stronger jolt than the original powder.

The practice—and extreme dangers—of freebasing first came to public attention in June 1980, when the popular comedian and film star Richard Pryor set himself on fire trying to freebase cocaine. The cocaine and ether mixture he was using exploded, setting even the hair on his chest ablaze. Pryor nearly died.

CRACK—THE DRUG OF THE '80s

In 1983 a new drug turned up in the Bahamas, a small island country off the eastern coast of Florida. Called crack, it was a form of freebased crystallized cocaine, cut (or mixed) with a substanced called "comeback" and baking soda.

Serious drug abusers are attracted to crack for two main reasons. First, it gives the kick of freebased cocaine, without the trouble and risk of freebasing the powder. And second, because the actual cocaine in crack is cut with less expensive substances, it is cheap. Enough crack for a half-hour jolt can be bought for as little as three dollars.

Unfortunately, crack is not only more powerful than ordinary cocaine, but also more addictive—and more deadly. Nevertheless, crack tore through the Bahamas like a tropical hurricane. From there it quickly jumped to the United States.

The first arrest involving crack in New York City came in 1985. Within a few years, crack had spread across America. By the late '80s, there were crackhouses in every big city and in many smaller ones. By 1989, as Senator Daniel Patrick Moynihan put it, an "epidemic [of] freebase cocaine abuse" had hit the United States. It is still raging.

As the 1990s began, a new fad was alarming antidrug officials. It was the increasing use of heroin and crack together. Abusers reported that the heroin mellowed the high they got from crack and made its effects last longer.

NEW DRUGS

The drugs discussed so far are not the only dangerous drugs in use in the United States today. In fact, it would be impossible to list all the illegal drugs now being abused. New drugs are being invented all the time. Among them are many so-called designer drugs, with names like China White and Ecstasy.

But the most disturbing of all the new drugs is the one known as "ice," or "L.A. glass." This extra-powerful form of methamphetamine from Japan turned up in Hawaii in the late 1980s. It may be the strongest of all the street drugs, new or old. It creates wild mood swings in many of its users, and sometimes the illusion of hearing voices as well. And, unfortunately, it frequently causes violent and irrational behavior.

Some abusers in Hawaii became so paranoid that they hid out in their homes for weeks or even months. They refused to leave for any reason except to buy new supplies of the drug.

By 1990s ice was showing up on the streets of West Coast cities like Los Angeles and Seattle, and even as far east as Boston. The first illegal laboratory for making ice was discovered in California in January 1990. Authorities suspected it was only one of many ice labs springing up across the country. They feared that ice would turn out to be "the drug of the '90's," just as cocaine had been the "drug of the '80s."

THE EXTENT OF AMERICA'S DRUG PROBLEM

In order to understand the role drugs play in American social and economic life, we can compare what Americans spend on them to what we spend on other things. Putting the official U.S. government estimate of $110 billion spent for illegal drugs next to U.S. Census Bureau figures of other consumer spending reveals some shocking realities.

The first is that we Americans spend over three times as much for illegal drugs as we do for legal ones!

The United States has been called the land of the automobile. It is said that we are in love with our cars. And yet we spend more for illegal drugs than we do for automobiles.

We spend four times as much for drugs as for jewelry and watches.

The comparison between what we spend on illegal drugs and what we spend on other forms of "recreation" is even more lopsided. We spend twice as much for illegal drugs as we do for all our television sets, radios, records, and musical instruments combined; over nine times as much as we spend for admission to all the movies, plays, operas, and rock concerts we attend each year; eleven times as much as we spend for books. And—despite the fact that Americans are said to be sports crazy—we spend over eighteen times as much for illegal drugs as we do to go to all the professional and amateur sporting events in the country put together.

But is America's drug problem getting better, or worse? It is hard to find a clear answer to that question. The reality seems to be that it is moving in both directions at once.

Today's 14.5 million drug users are actually fewer than the 23 million or so who used them in 1985. But this drop in total numbers does not necessarily mean that America's problem with drugs is getting less serious. Although fewer people are experimenting with illegal drugs, a higher proportion of those who do are becoming heavy abusers.

To some extent, this increase in serious abusers may be due to the fact that drugs are getting more powerful, and more addictive, all the time. Crack is more addictive than ordinary cocaine. And ice may be the most dangerous and destructive drug yet. Even cannabis, the mildest of the popular drugs, is more powerful than it used to be.

Most of the illicit drugs used in the United States come from somewhere else. Of the three most-often abused drugs—marijuana, heroin, and cocaine—only marijuana is widely produced in the United States. And even the bulk of the marijuana used in the United States is imported. In the next chapter we will examine the vast international trade that brings these destructive commodities to our shores.

CHAPTER FIVE

IMPORTING

DEATH

THE international drug trade is a business—a very big business. Unfortunately, there is no way to tell exactly how big a business it really is. The criminal organizations that run the drug trade don't open their books for outsiders to look at. Drug smugglers don't itemize their cargoes on customs forms. And the pushers who peddle drugs on the street don't report their illegal earnings on their income-tax returns.

The drug trade is not the biggest industry in the world, but it may be the most profitable. Drug profits are based on some very simple economic facts. The ingredients that go into illegal drugs cost very little, and the market for them is enormous.

Although the ingredients are cheap, there *are* some significant expenses involved in the drug trade. They include the costs of manufacturing the drugs, smuggling them, protecting them from other dealers, and bribing corrupt police officials. But these costs are relatively small when compared to the expenses of most honest businesses. And, unlike honest businesspeople, the traffickers don't pay taxes on the money they make from the drug trade.

Like food, all three of the most widely abused drugs begin as agricultural commodities. Marijuana comes from the cannabis plant. Heroin comes from the opium poppy. And cocaine comes from the coca leaf. In general, the people who actually grow these plants receive very little money for their produce. But almost everyone else involved in the illegal drug traffic—except, of course, the drug abusers, their families, and the victims of their crimes—makes a lot of money.

THE CUSTOMERS

Illegal drugs of one sort or another are used almost everywhere in the world. And drug use is spreading, even into areas that once had little or no problem with drugs. For the first time in modern history, for example, Egypt is showing signs of a serious drug problem. Drug use even seems to be on the increase in the previously tightly controlled societies of Eastern Europe.

Hungary was already estimated to have at least 30,000 addicts by the mid-1980s; Poland, somewhere between 200,000 and 600,000. AIDS has become as serious a threat to Eastern European heroin users as it is for those in the West. The train running from West Berlin to Warsaw in Poland has become known as the "AIDS express" because so much heroin is smuggled in it.

The Soviet Union admitted to having 46,000 drug addicts back in 1987. But the fact that it also claimed arrests of 4,000 drug dealers in a single crackdown suggests that the real number of users must be much higher than that. Most Soviet addicts are hooked on opium, or on a variety of cannabis called "anashi." Both are homegrown. So far, it seems, the international drug traders have not made a dent in the Soviet market. But that may change. With the breakdown of barriers between the East and the West, Eastern Europe and the Soviet Union may soon be as vulnerable to the international drug trade as the Western countries. Drug use there is likely to soar in the 1990s.

But the real focus of the world's drug trade remains on the great North American market, made up of the United States and Canada. About 60 percent of all the illegal drugs used in the entire world are used there. Estimates of the money spent on illicit drugs in the United States alone start at $100 billion a year. And they go up from there. The Bush administration puts the figure at $110 billion. Others put it as high as $200 billion. Even the government's estimate is more than twice the value of all the food products the United States exports and imports combined. That means that drugs are a more important element of America's international trade than food!

THE CANNABIS TRADE

During the 1960s, most of the marijuana and hashish smuggled into the United States was brought by amateurs. Many professional drug smugglers, who dealt in heroin and other hard drugs, were not interested in the relatively bulky and less profitable cannabis. Those who were could not keep up with the skyrocketing demand.

Most of the amateurs got started smuggling small amounts of pot from nearby Mexico. "Acapulco gold" was available and cheap on the streets of Mexican border towns. It was especially cheap for those who paid for it with U.S. dollars. The Mexican economy was poor, and the Mexican peso kept losing value. But the U.S. dollar was considered to be as good as gold—even Acapulco gold.

All a would-be American drug dealer had to do was drive across the Mexican border. In a single sunny afternoon in Tijuana or Ciudad Juarez, an American could buy as much pot as he or she had money for. Hiding it in the spare tire of a car or in the false bottom of a suitcase, the smuggler could usually pass back across the border without a problem. And that's exactly what a lot of hippies, college students, and small-time criminals did.

Returning to their hometowns—or to college towns like Columbus, Ohio, and Madison, Wisconsin—most of them would simply sell their smuggled pot to their friends. The more ambitious of these amateur smugglers, however, would turn professional. Instead of a single trip, they'd take many. Instead of just selling to friends, they'd organize those friends into a network of dealers. Those dealers would sell to an ever widening circle of their own friends and acquaintances, and eventually to strangers as well. Some of these enterprising young smugglers used their profits to put themselves through college. Others founded substantial criminal enterprises.

In her book *Desperados*, Elaine Shannon mentions a group of San Diego high school students who began smuggling pot in the 1960s. By the time they were caught in the 1980s, they had made about $100 million.

Many of the young marijuana dealers of the '60s never took their criminal activities seriously *as* criminal activities. Most dealt only in pot, never in the harder drugs. They knew that pot was against the law, of course, but they thought it was a silly law. To them, and to their friends, there was nothing morally wrong with using pot. Therefore, they told themselves, there was nothing morally wrong with smuggling pot either.

Some got away with their criminal activities, but many others got caught. During much of the '60s, however, the criminal penalties for dealing in marijuana were not strictly enforced, particularly against middle-class young people with no previous record. The lucky ones got off with probation and a small fine (small to a drug dealer with a profitable business). But not everyone was so lucky. Several of those who got caught spent years in prison.

Even in the 1960s, not everyone who traded in marijuana was an amateur. The big profits made in pot soon attracted more hardened criminals. Many of the '60s-style amateurs got out of the business when they started coming in conflict with more traditional—and vicious—criminal organizations. These included branches of the American Mafia, as well as foreign gangs from Mexico, Colombia, Jamaica, and elsewhere.

Those amateurs who stayed became professionals themselves. They included such people as David Steinberg, whose story is told in James Mills's book *The Underground Empire*. A young man from suburban Illinois, Steinberg turned his small-time smuggling business into a multimillion dollar operation in just a few years.

A British equivalent of Steinberg was Dennis Howard Marks. He, too, began his smuggling career as an amateur in the '60s, supplying the students at England's Oxford University with pot in much the same way young Americans were supplying their college towns with "Acapulco gold."

By the 1980s Marks had built his organization into one of the biggest marijuana smuggling operations in the world. By the time he was caught, in Spain in 1988, his operations extended around the world. He was even supplying about 15 percent of the foreign cannabis coming into the United States. Neither Marks nor Steinberg had remained amateurs for long. Nevertheless, they prided themselves on avoiding the viciousness and killings associated with more traditional drug smugglers.

The same cannot be said of the major criminal organizations that import and distribute marijuana in the United States today. They are as large, professional, and vicious as any of the gangs that smuggle heroin or cocaine around the world. In fact, they are often the same organizations.

Much of today's drug trade is carried out by cartels— associations of drug traffickers joined together to control the supply of drugs. Some cartels are formed to control a particular drug or drugs. Others are formed to control the production or distribution of drugs in a certain part of the world.

In 1984 Mexican authorities claimed a great victory in their battle against a marijuana cartel centered around Guadalajara, Mexico. They announced that they had arrested more than 170 people and seized more than 20 tons of marijuana, hashish oil, and cannabis seed. In addition, they had found and destroyed about 150 acres of cannabis fields.

The Guadalajara cartel was an important player in the U.S. marijuana trade. Tons of its product were exported to the United States every year. But the cartel did not limit itself to marijuana. It was also a force in the Mexican-U.S. cocaine and heroin markets. What is more, it was so large and effective that the 1984 raids did little to hinder its operations. Early the next year, DEA Agent Enrique Camarena was investigating the marijuana operations of the Guadalajara cartel when he became the first U.S. law-enforcement official to be killed in President Ronald Reagan's war on drugs. The cartel is still functioning and still shipping its various poisons into the United States. And it is just one of many.

THE HEROIN TRADE

Following World War II, the heroin trade was dominated by two professional criminal organizations. Each of them was based on a different island in the Mediterranean Sea. The best known of the two was the Mafia, or Cosa Nostra, from Sicily. This secret brotherhood had branches in several countries. The most important, outside of Sicily, was the one in the United States.

The second major organization was a Corsican gang with strong ties to a French dockworkers' union. (The island of Corsica is a part of France.) It also had ties to the French secret service and perhaps to its American cousin, the OSS (Office of Strategic Services).

In the first decades after the war, the Corsicans dominated the heroin trade. Their main business involved smuggling Iranian opium to secret laboratories in the French port city of Marseilles, where it was converted into heroin. With their control of the Marseilles docks, they were easily able to ship their product throughout Europe, and even to the United States.

Eventually, the government of Iran put an end to the sale of Iranian opium poppies. But the Corsicans had other sources to choose from. Turkey, for one, had large poppy crops available. Another source was Southeast Asia, much of which was then the

French colony of Indochina. At that time, in the 1950s, the French were engaged in a struggle against revolutionaries who were determined to drive them out of the region.

By the 1960s the French battle for Indochina had turned into America's war in Vietnam. As we have seen, the American presence in Vietnam produced a surge in American demand for heroin. But it did more than that for the heroin trade. It gave American criminals new access to Southeast Asian opium.

Even while the Corsicans dominated much of the heroin trade, the Sicilian Mafia remained active. The Mafia had some advantages of its own, including a better network for distributing the drug in some parts of the world. One of them was the United States.

In America, as elsewhere, the Mafia was divided into "families." The families had close ties to one another, as well as to the original Mafia back in Sicily. But each family was also a separate organization. It had its own boss, or godfather, and its own territory—a geographical area in which it controlled Mafia activities. One family had control of activities in Philadelphia, for instance, another in Milwaukee, another in Detroit, and so on. New York was divided between five different families, but each had its own area of criminal responsibility. Occasionally, "wars" would break out between families. In general, however, a "commission" of godfathers tried to settle disputes between families peacefully, in a way that would profit the Cosa Nostra as a whole.

As an institution, the American Mafia frowned on the drug traffic in the 1950s. Many of the families were reluctant to participate in it at all. Ironically, some godfathers claimed to have moral objections to dealing in drugs. Others simply felt that getting involved in the drug traffic would bring them more trouble than it was worth.

Despite this, some families did deal in drugs, even in the '50s. Then, during the drug craze of the 1960s, drug profits became too big for most of the families to pass up. Within a few years, the Mafia had established control of most heroin distribution in the United States. Much of the heroin it distributed, however, came from the Corsican laboratories in Marseilles. This link between the two criminal organizations became known as the French Connection.

Most of the American heroin supply was made from Turkish poppies. In those days the farmers in Turkey were legally licensed to grow opium poppies for sale to the legal drug companies. But many Turkish farmers were selling their poppies to manufacturers in Lebanon. The Lebanese turned them into morphine, from which heroin could be made. They then sold the morphine to the French Connection laboratories in Marseilles.

Then, in 1973, President Richard Nixon declared the first "war on drugs." It was directed mostly against a single enemy, heroin, and it was fought almost entirely by diplomatic means. (There was also an effort to cut off the flow of Mexican marijuana into the United States. It caused such a traffic jam at the border that it was quickly dropped.) For a short time the war against heroin was successful. By putting economic pressure on the government of Turkey, the United States managed to choke off the supply of Turkish opium.

Even before that, the French Connection had been badly damaged by some fiercely effective police work in both New York and France. Many, if not most, of the laboratories in Marseilles were closed down. The story of the investigation that led to the downfall of the alliance was told in Robin Moore's book, *The French Connection*, in 1969. The book was made into a movie that won the Academy Award for Best Picture in 1971.

But, in the long run, the war on heroin was a failure. Cutting off Turkish opium only caused the price of the drug to soar. Eager to profit from the higher price, the criminals looked to the East, where the Golden Triangle was more than ready to make up for the loss of Golden Crescent poppies.

One source was the Hmong tribes who lived in the mountains of Laos. The Hmong tribes were friendly to the American effort in Southeast Asia, and they willingly fought the Communists to help the Americans. But they needed to support themselves while they were fighting. Opium was one of the few cash crops they could grow where they lived. Amazingly, despite the president's war on drugs, the American CIA (Central Intelligence Agency) apparently encouraged the Hmongs to grow opium poppies to support themselves. The opium was sold to traffickers in Thailand and elsewhere, where it was made available for the American and European market. Theoretically, the heroin was not meant to find its way to the United States. It was supposed to remain in Asia or be shipped to Europe or elsewhere. (The CIA was apparently unconcerned about the destruction the drug would cause in other countries.) But, as it turned out, much of this U.S.-sponsored opium did find its way into the veins of American addicts.

There is evidence that some of the same CIA planes that flew weapons and military supplies into the Hmong's mountain strongholds in Laos carried opium out. Earlier the CIA had also helped the Chinese anti-Communist guerrillas who supported themselves by growing opium in northern Burma.

Before long, drug traffickers were all but buried under new supplies, not only from Southeast Asia, but from India, Pakistan, and elsewhere in the Golden Crescent as well. Hungry for customers, they began to develop new markets in Australia and Europe. They were wildly successful. According to Professor Al McCoy, a leading expert on the international drug trade, the number of drug addicts in Holland, for example, was multiplied by 10 between 1973 and 1976.

Meanwhile, the Sicilian Mafia was cashing in on the new opportunities opening up in the United States. In his book *Last Days of the Sicilians*, Ralph Blumenthal describes how the Mafia set up its own heroin factories in Italy in the 1970s and increased its exports to the United States.

Even long after the war in Vietnam ended, the flow of opium from the Golden Crescent to the Mafia's Italian factories continued. By the 1980s Iranian poppy production was booming again. Production was even booming in Afghanistan, despite the war between the Communist government, aided by Soviet troops, and Mujahadin rebels.

Once again there was an ironic connection between the U.S.

government and foreign opium growers. The American government was sending weapons and other aid to the Mujahadin rebels, even though some of them were helping to pay for their fight against the Communists by growing opium poppies.

With a steadily growing supply of opium, the Sicilian Mafia set up a network of its own to distribute heroin in the United States. It used pizza parlors in cities across the country as covers for its real business. When the FBI eventually broke up the Sicilians' network in 1984, the newspapers jokingly called the investigation "the Pizza Connection" case.

The breakup of the Pizza Connection badly damaged the Mafia's drug business. Like the earlier breakup of the French Connection, it even reduced the supply of heroin for a short time. But it did little to reduce demand for the drug.

In the wake of the FBI crackdown, the Mafia was unable to supply the growing number of desperate addicts. This opened the way for other gangs of organized criminals to grab a share of the American market. The majority of these new suppliers were Chinese, or Americans of Chinese descent. Chinese-American gangs had long distributed drugs in the Chinese neighborhoods of American and Canadian cities. Now they began branching out.

Law-enforcement officials are still not sure just who these new suppliers are. There seem to be many different groups involved. They range from street gangs to much larger and more sophisticated organizations. The FBI suspects that some of the gangs may be branches of the notorious triads—traditional Chinese criminal brotherhoods that are even older and more secretive than the Sicilian Mafia. The DEA is not so sure. But whoever they are, and wherever they come from, the new gangs have good contacts in Hong Kong, Taiwan, and the Golden Triangle itself.

Some of those contacts probably include the Communist guerrillas in northeast Burma, who now grow poppies in the same fields where the anti-Communist guerrillas once grew them. Other contacts may include high officials of at least some Southeast Asian governments. Al McCoy has suggested that the

Laotian government, for one, "appears to be participating, at least quasi-officially, in the narcotics traffic."

By 1987 law-enforcement officials were already estimating that Chinese or Chinese-American gangs controlled about 40 percent of the heroin entering New York City. That percentage has almost certainly been going up ever since. With the large numbers of Chinese-Americans who live in the big cities on the West Coast, the gangs probably control an even larger slice of the heroin market there.

Lately there are signs that the Chinese gangs may not be the only Asian gangs heavily involved in heroin distribution in the United States. There are rumors that a Vietnamese gang is entering the American market as well. One group that does *not* seem to be involved, according to McCoy, is the Hmong refugees in America. They were never heavily into the production or distribution of heroin, even in Asia. They were merely farmers who grew poppies as a cash crop.

THE VOLCANO THAT RAINS DOWN COCAINE

Coca is grown in India and parts of Asia, as well as in South America. But most of the coca that ends up as cocaine in the United States is grown in the Andes mountains of South America, particularly in Bolivia and Peru. The Andes contain many volcanoes, some of which are constantly active, raining ash and molten lava down on the surrounding countryside. But none is more active—or more deadly—than the volcano of cocaine that rains suffering and death down on the people of the world.

Peru is by far the world's largest producer of coca. Its major growing region, the Huallaga Valley, produces nearly 60 percent of all the cocaine that enters the United States. Another 20 percent comes from Bolivia. The rest comes from a handful of other countries, including Colombia and Mexico.

Coca has been grown in Peru for thousands of years. It was

traditionally used as a mild stimulant, although some super-stitious Peruvians believed its leaves had magical powers, in much the same way as some Europeans believe herbs can cast spells or that tea leaves can foretell the future.

Some of the Andean crop is still grown to be used in these traditional ways. The rest is bought by drug traffickers. They convert the leaves into cocaine paste, which is less bulky and easier to carry. Most of the paste is smuggled into Peru's neighbor to the north, Colombia, where it ends up in the hands of several cartels that operate there. It is in their illegal "factories" that the paste is converted into the powdered cocaine that is so white that it is sometimes known as "snow."

Altogether, Andean coca leaves supply about 400 tons of cocaine a year—a total that is going up. About 200 tons of that end up in the United States. The rest is shipped to Europe. Andean coca eventually sells for something like $100 billion on the streets of cities around the world. And yet, says Peru's ambassador to the United States, Cesar Atala-Nazal, the average Peruvian peasant farmer gets only $1,000 for his entire crop. According to Atala-Nazal, that's not much more than he could get for other crops, such as coffee.

Most Peruvian farmers have few moral qualms about growing coca. It is a legal crop in Peru, when it is grown for traditional uses. Even so, says Atala-Nazal, many farmers feel uncomfort-able selling their crop to drug traffickers. They would rather not deal with criminals. But the average farmer is so poor that even the small difference between the price of coca and the price of coffee can mean the difference between relative comfort and real suffering for his wife and children.

This is even truer for the peasant farmers of Bolivia. Bolivia is both smaller and poorer than Peru. Peru has roughly 22 million people, with a per capita income of about $1,000. Bolivia has fewer than 7 million people, and its per capita income is only $536. Because of this, even though Bolivia grows much less coca than Peru, coca is even more important to Bolivia's economy. In fact, according to the Bolivian ambassador to the United States, coca accounts for about 20 percent of the country's total income.

In "jungle labs" like this one in Peru, coca leaves are prepared for the next step in the cocaine trade.

What is more, about 20 percent of Bolivia's workers owe their jobs to the coca trade—and that means to the cocaine trade.

THE DRUG LORDS

In recent decades the cocaine trade has been controlled largely by the Colombian cartels. Colombia's position on the northwest edge of South America makes it ideal for anyone interested in manufacturing cocaine. It is conveniently located between the coca-growing countries to the South and the fabulously rich cocaine markets to the North. In between are countries like Panama and Mexico, which have provided no serious obstacles to drug smuggling in the past.

There are four large Colombian cartels and several smaller ones. They are known by the names of the places in which they are based. Of the big four, the Medellín, Cali, and Bogotá cartels are named for cities. The fourth is named for Colombia's North Coast region.

The cartel that gets the most attention in the press is the one whose headquarters are in the manufacturing city of Medellín, in west-central Colombia. Although it is the best known of all the cartels, it is not the one that supplies the most cocaine to the United States. That is the Cali cartel, which, alone, accounts for about 40 percent of the U.S. supply. The $20 billion worth of cocaine found in the September 1989 DEA raid near Los Angeles belonged to the Cali cartel.

Like the others, the Medellín cartel was formed by an alliance between several separate crime organizations. Most of them were profitable businesses, run either by ruthless and determined individuals or by families. Unlike the American Mafia, the cartels are often real family businesses, with fathers, brothers, sons (and sometimes sisters and daughters as well) all working together.

The leading figures in the founding of the Medellín cartel were Pablo Escobar, Carlos Lehder, and several members of the Rodriguez and Ochoa families. Such men are sometimes referred to as "drug lords." But they are "lordly" only in the sense that they consider themselves to be above the laws and moral concerns that govern the actions of other people. They claim the right to kill and to destroy anyone and anything that gets in their way.

The Colombian cocaine cartels are among the most murderous, and merciless, criminal organizations on Earth. Judges who dare to prosecute them in Colombian courts are not just liable to be murdered; they are likely to be killed in front of their own children. In order to kill a few "snitches" who had informed against them—and to send a message to others who might be tempted to snitch in the future—the cartels blew up a whole passenger plane. The bomb, which destroyed an Avianca jetliner on November 17, 1989, killed not only the 5 informers, but 102 completely uninvolved people who happened to be flying from Bogotá to Cali on the same flight.

"NARCOTERRORISM"

The best illustration of just how ruthless and powerful the cartels can be came in 1980. At that time the Medellín cartel came into conflict with the revolutionary Communist guerrilla force known as M-19. A ruthless and powerful organization in itself, M-19 was considered by international law-enforcement officials to be one of the most vicious terrorist organizations in the world. Its guerrillas haunted the Colombian jungles, emerging at will to strike with merciless brutality at the nation's right-wing politicians and business leaders. Among other atrocities, they were responsible for the killing of 11 Colombian Supreme Court judges in 1985.

M-19 was considered to be the most intimidating group of outlaws in all of Colombia—until it encountered the Medellín cartel. Along with armed robbery, ransom was one of the M-19's most dependable sources of income. But, in 1980, it made the mistake of kidnapping two women members of the Ochoa family. The enraged cartel determined to teach the Communist rebels a lesson.

Ramon Millan-Rodriguez, who was then an employee of the cartel, later went before a committee of the United States Congress to describe what happened. The cartel was aware, he said, that the M-19 was incredibly cruel. As he put it, the rebels had people who were willing to use a child to shield them from bullets. In order to defeat them, cartel leaders knew, they would need people who were "willing to shoot through the child." It found them. In fact, it hired what Millan-Rodriguez described as 2,000 "sociopaths" to do battle with the M-19. Within a few weeks, the cartel's private army had brought the feared M-19 guerrillas to their knees.

According to Millan-Rodriguez, the cartel could have easily wiped out the M-19 altogether. Instead, it made a deal with the guerrillas. The M-19 was spared. In return, the women were returned safely, and without ransom. From that point on, the two groups—the Medellín cartel and M-19—worked together. The cartel helped to fund M-19, while M-19 helped to protect the cartel's drug business. This alliance between the two groups spawned a new term for a new kind of criminal enterprise—"narcoterrorism."

"MULES"

Between them, the Colombian cartels ship billions of dollars worth of cocaine to the United States every year. It comes into the country in a variety of ways. It is flown in on private airplanes that land at secret airstrips scattered about the American South, or it is dropped from the sky. It is smuggled in the cargoos of ships and planes and in the luggage of innocent-looking tourists.

"Mules," disguised as ordinary travelers, carry packages of cocaine taped to their skin—or even hidden *inside* their bodies. When a Colombian Avianca jetliner crashed on Long Island in early 1990, several passengers survived. One passenger who was lucky enough to survive the crash was unlucky enough to require surgery. When the surgeons opened up his stomach during the operation, they found several sausagelike packages filled with cocaine. Checking other survivors, they found similar packets in another passenger.

The discovery was not surprising to customs officials. "Mules" have been found with as many as 95 such packages in their stomachs and intestines. It was not surprising to doctors in major port cities, either. Ruptured cocaine packets are often found during autopsies performed on international travelers who die suddenly. When a packet of pure cocaine breaks open inside a smuggler's body, death from cocaine poisoning almost always follows.

Once inside the United States, a load of cocaine is distributed by one or more of hundreds of drug-trafficking "cells." Each of these relatively small organizations is run by a Colombian who works for the cartels. According to a cover story in *Newsweek* magazine, the FBI has identified about 300 of these Colombian-run cells in cities across the country. There are probably many, many more.

The cartels' representatives do not actually sell drugs on the street. For one thing, a Colombian drug dealer would stick out like a sore thumb in most American neighborhoods, from the white suburbs to the black ghettos. For another, there is not enough profit in street sales. Instead, the cartel's representatives act more as brokers than as salesmen. They market the smuggled drugs to a network of American dealers, collect the profits, and send them home to Colombia.

In big cities, cocaine is often sold by local gangs, such as the Crips and the Bloods in Los Angeles, and the Brothers of Struggle in Milwaukee. They know the streets, and they have enough organization to handle the large volume of drugs and money involved.

MONEY "LAUNDERING"

Most big, legal businesses rarely use cash. They use checks, bank transfers, computer entries, or other sophisticated ways of moving money that do not require the handling of many actual bills and coins. Large amounts of cash are just too clumsy to deal with.

The illegal drug business is an exception to the rule. Most drug deals, large and small, are made in cash. The Colombian cartel demands cash from the gang leader who buys a truckload of cocaine, just as the drug pusher demands cash from the stranger who buys an ounce of marijuana from him on the street.

There are two main reasons for relying on cash. The first is that drug dealers do not trust each other. They are criminals, and they know better than most that there is no honor among thieves—particularly where money is concerned.

The second reason is the fact that cash leaves no record. Other kinds of financial transactions leave a trail of paper evidence: bills of sale, entries in account books, bank statements, and so on. Following the paper trail left by drug money is one of the most effective ways authorities have of nailing major drug traffickers. What is more, when the authorities can identify money or other assets resulting from drug deals, they can seize them. All of this makes cash an attractive alternative to other kinds of large financial transactions for drug dealers.

But always dealing in cash means that traffickers often find themselves with huge amounts of it on their hands. Just how huge was demonstrated in January 1989 when DEA agents raided a warehouse in Queens, New York. The warehouse supposedly belonged to a company called Zoom Furniture. But Zoom was actually a front for some of the Cali drug cartel's operations in the United States. Inside, the DEA found $19 million in cash.

Having millions of dollars in cash may not seem like a big problem to most of us, but for a drug trafficker, it presents several different problems at once. Millions of dollars in cash are incredibly bulky just to carry around. That much money is hard to conceal, and its presence is a great temptation to thieves. What is worse, cash earns no interest. Money is most valuable when it is put to work: when it is invested in a bank or in a profitable business, where it makes more money while waiting to be spent.

American cash money presents still another problem to foreign drug traffickers. They have to find ways to convert it into their own currency before they can spend it in their native countries. It is impossible simply to exchange large amounts of U.S. dollars for Colombian pesos (or Iranian rials, or Thai bahts) without attracting a lot of attention. And attention is exactly what drug traffickers want to avoid.

For all these reasons, drug traffickers want to be able to put their money into banks and to shift it around the world, just like other international businesspeople do. But drug money is dirty. It is tainted by the fact that it comes from an illegal enterprise. This means that it has to be "laundered." That is, it has to be handled in ways that conceal its source.

There are many elaborate schemes to launder money. Most of them involve transferring large amounts of money between various front corporations. Typically, a major dealer, or cartel, will establish several companies. Some may be real business enterprises. Others may be nothing more than "shell" companies—corporations that do little or no actual business. They are usually registered in countries whose laws make it easy for businesses to conceal not only their real ownership but the true nature of their operations as well.

The dealers open bank accounts in the name of the phony businesses. Sometimes one company will have several accounts in several different countries. Drug money is deposited in one of these accounts, then moved back and forth between the various accounts and corporations. The object is to make the money trail too complicated for anyone to follow.

When the money is "washed clean" enough, it is all but impossible to trace in either direction. No investigator, starting on the trail of money from a drug deal, can follow it to its final destination in the bank account of an international drug lord. And no investigator, starting from the bank account of a drug lord, can prove that the money in it came from drugs.

Several countries around the world play key roles in international money laundering. Laws in the Bahamas, the Isle of Man in the Irish Sea, and the Pacific island chain of Vanuatu, among other places, make it easy to set up shell corporations. Hong Kong is a major banking center for the Asian drug rings, who smuggle heroin to North America and American money back to Asia. In recent decades, Australia has become an important center for laundering heroin money. And, at least until the 1989 U.S. invasion, the Central American country of Panama was the main money center for the Colombian cartels. Since then, some of the money that used to go through Panama has been rerouted through Uruguay in South America.

But the real heart of the international drug trade is still in North America. This is where most of the money paid for drugs comes from, and this is where the first cycle of the laundry process begins. Los Angeles, Toronto, Canada, and, most of all, New York City are all major drug money laundering centers.

Some banks, particularly in those countries with helpful banking laws, are little more than money laundries. They are established primarily for that purpose. But much of the money laundering goes on in apparently respectable mainstream banks as well, both in the United States and abroad. In Panama, for example, there is evidence that a lot of cartel money was laundered in Panamanian branches of U.S. banks, such as Citibank and the Bank of America. Ramon Millan-Rodriguez has testified that he laundered many millions of dollars in "respectable" banks, whose officers knew very well who they were dealing with.

For many years the U.S. government has required banks to report all cash transactions of $10,000 or more. For a while, the reporting requirement made drug traffickers cautious. They hired "smurfs" to make scores of bank deposits for them, each deposit adding up to just under the amount that would have to be reported. But the sheer amount of drug money became so great that traffickers began throwing caution to the winds.

In 1984 only 704,521 transactions over $10,000 were reported. By 1986 the number had risen to 3,563,986. By 1988, the last year for which totals are available, the number had soared to 5,743,942. The government simply did not have enough investigators to check on even a small proportion of these millions of transactions. Nevertheless, in early 1990 the government lowered the size of the transactions that had to be reported, from $10,000 to $3,000. Probably only a fraction of such transactions involve drug money. For the already overworked federal investigators who are trying to find out which ones those are, it is like looking for an unknown number of ordinary-looking trees in a very large forest.

Drug trafficking is a crime that breeds other crimes. In the next chapter we will explore the scourge of violence and corruption the drug trade has unleased in the United States.

CHAPTER SIX

CRIME IN
THE STREETS—
AND IN THE HOME

ILLEGAL drugs have been compared to a plague—a terrible and contagious disease, like the Black Death that terrorized Europe in the fourteenth century. Like the Black Death, drugs sweep through a society, striking down people of all ages and social conditions. But drugs are worse than any plague. A plague is a single disease. It sickens and kills in just one way. Drugs find many ways to kill. And they do more than strike down individuals. They infect and undermine the health of the whole society.

When the drug plague struck the United States, it brought an epidemic of crime along with it. In some ways, this side effect of the drug plague has been just as bad as—or even worse than— the original disease. It has turned the streets of our big cities into battlegrounds, corrupted politicians and law enforcement officials, disrupted our courts, overcrowded our prisons, and threatened the very values that once held our society together.

THE CRIME EXPLOSION

In the view of Mayor David Dinkins of New York City, the drug problem "is primarily a crisis in public safety." And that crisis is getting worse all the time. It is most urgent in the nation's cities, where drug use is the most widespread.

In 1988, the last full year reported by the FBI, the national crime rate was up 2.1 percent over 1987. But the rate for violent crimes—the robberies, aggravated assaults, and murders most often associated with drugs—was up 4.5 percent. That means that there were more than 637 violent crimes for every 100,000 men, women, and children in the United States. In the first six months of 1989, the crime rate rose again, up about 3 percent in the country as a whole. And in the cities, it was exploding. In the 39 cities with populations of more than 100,000, the rate of violent crimes soared over 19 percent. In 9 of those cities, it was up more than 20 percent. In Philadelphia, for example, it was up 21 percent; in Little Rock, Arkansas, almost 22 percent.

According to law-enforcement officials, most—if not all—of this rise in the crime rate was due to drugs. A lot of evidence supports this claim. In New York City, everyone who is arrested and booked is tested for drug use. By late 1989, 83 percent were testing positive. Fifty-three percent of the men arrested in Dallas, Texas, were testing positive for cocaine. And so were 51 percent of the women. According to the U.S. Justice Department, suspects in typical cities across the country were averaging between 53 percent and 79 percent positive for drugs.

DRUG-RELATED KILLINGS

The link between drugs and the rise in crime is most dramatic in the case of violent crimes—especially the most terrible of all crimes, murder. Four hundred and thirty-eight people were murdered in Washington, D.C., in 1989—a new record for the city. The previous record had been set only the year before, when 369 people were killed. Most of the victims were either shot or stabbed to death. According to Washington police, over 60 percent of these murders involved drugs or drug use.

Washington's high rate of drug-related murders is typical of America's big cities. Detroit had 623 murders in 1989, up from 586 the year before. Los Angeles had 834, up from the previous year's 736. Police in both cities stated that the majority of the killings were drug-related.

A murder is generally classified as drug-related if it is committed to get drugs, or money for drugs; if it takes place during a drug transaction; if either the killer or the victim is a drug dealer, or is using drugs at the time of the crime.

The first thing many people imagine when they think of drug-*related* violence is drug-*induced* violence; that is, an act of violence committed by someone who is crazed by drugs. And it is true that some incredibly brutal crimes are committed by people while in the psychotic state produced by certain drugs. A man on crack attacks his wife or children. A hallucinating LSD user lashes out at friends with a knife, believing they are great green monsters coming to carry him away. A woman on mescaline hears voices that tell her to kill her newborn infant— and she does. When events like these occur, they receive a lot of attention in the media. But such events are relatively rare, compared to other kinds of drug-related killings.

Many drug-related killings are the result of drug deals gone bad. A supplier cheats a dealer, and the angry dealer kills him. Or vice versa. A desperate addict tries to steal drugs from a fellow addict, a fight breaks out, and one or the other is killed. Two groups of criminals set up a meeting, in which one group is to buy drugs from another. But instead of bringing the money, the supposed buyers bring guns, kill the would-be sellers, and steal the drugs. Or the supposed sellers bring guns instead of drugs, kill the would-be buyers, and steal the money. And so on.

Other killings take place over turf. Street dealers often

In the front lines on the war on drugs, U.S. marshals carry out a raid on a suspected crack house in Washington, D.C.

quarrel over the "right" to sell on a particular street, or even on a particular street corner. Interviewed on the *MacNeil/Lehrer* television program, Deputy Chief Glen Levant of the Los Angeles Police Department claimed that on some street corners there, 10 to 15 drug dealers sometimes jostle each other just to get to the cars of would-be cocaine buyers.

When gangs quarrel over which will control sales in a certain neighborhood or city, the stugggle often turns deadly. In Los Angeles, drive-by killings—in which members of drug-dealing gangs shoot down rival gang members from passing automobiles—became common in the 1980s. According to Dallas Police Chief Mack Vines, from 60 to 70 of the 367 murders that took place in Dallas last year involved Jamaican drug-dealing gangs.

Unfortunately, it is not just gang members and other drug dealers who get killed when the criminals start shooting each other. Innocent people often die as well. Even small children sometimes get caught in the crossfire. In Philadelphia a five-year-old boy named Marcus Yates was shot in the head during a shootout between drug dealers. It was not a rare event. In Los Angeles County, for example, there were 387 gang-related killings in 1987. About half of the dead were bystanders who just happened to get in the way.

STREET CRIMES

Drugs cost money. Addicts who are really hooked on drugs will do whatever they have to do to get the money to buy them. For a high school student in the suburbs, that might mean getting a part-time job in a fast-food restaurant. Or it might mean stealing from his or her mother's purse. For addicts in the inner cities, where the chances for a job are small, it very often means turning to the streets.

Many addicts become pushers themselves, earning the money to feed their own habits by selling drugs to others. Those who are young—including suburban and rural young people who have been driven from their homes—often turn to prostitution. Others, of all ages, turn to stealing, or to such violent crimes as muggings and armed robberies.

The numbers of such crimes have skyrocketed since the early 1960s, when drugs began to sweep through American society like a modern strain of the Black Death. According to FBI statistics, for example, there were 630 burglaries for every 100,000 people in 1963. In 1987 there were 1,602. In 1963 there were 74.2 robberies. In 1987 there were 315. And the numbers have climbed since then. Police authorities are convinced that *most* of these increases are accounted for by addicts, desperate for the money to buy drugs.

FAMILY VIOLENCE

Drugs don't just cause crime in the streets. They cause crime in the home as well. And that crime is often worse than anything street criminals can do. Violence carried out by strangers is terrible enough. But when we are subjected to violence from those we love, and who are supposed to love us, it is even more horrible.

At 6:35 on the morning of November 2, 1987, police officers arrived at the apartment of a former lawyer named Joel Steinberg in New York's Greenwich Village. They had been called there by a woman named Hedda Nussbaum, who had reported that a child was in trouble.

This was not the first time there had been trouble at that apartment. Joel Steinberg was a violent man, and neighbors suspected that he often physically abused Hedda and his two adopted children.

The building was well kept, attractive, and pleasant by Manhattan standards. Most of the tenants were middle-class, professional people. The author Mark Twain, who created the famous fictional children Tom Sawyer and Huckleberry Finn, once lived there.

But what the policeman found when he entered the Steinberg apartment was as far from pleasant as he could imagine. Moving past the protesting ex-lawyer and Hedda herself, he found one small child attached to a kind of leash. Not far away he found the unconscious body of a once very pretty little girl. She was lying on the floor with vomit coming out of her mouth. She had been terribly battered. Examining her, he found that she was still alive, but only barely. An ambulance was called, and she was rushed to a nearby hospital. But there was nothing the doctors could do. She died a few days later.

The little girl's name was Lisa Steinberg. She was six years old. Her death made headlines across the nation. It seemed too incredible, too horrible, for people to believe. It turned out that Joel Steinberg had been beating up Hedda Nussbaum for at least nine years. And after he had adopted Lisa, he'd taken to beating her too.

For several weeks the Steinberg case focused national attention on the question of child and spouse abuse. How could Joel Steinberg have been so cruel as to beat a defenseless child to death? How could an intelligent and educated woman have put up with Steinberg's repeated violence? Newspapers, magazines, and television programs interviewed expert after expert to find some explanation that everyone could understand. Psychologists talked about Steinberg's obvious emotional problems. Social critics talked about how men in America are raised to confuse violence with manliness. Feminists talked about the vulnerability of women in today's society, and about the "battered woman syndrome."

But DEA Agent Robert Stutman believes the real explanation of the Steinberg case was almost entirely overlooked. Whatever other factors contributed to the death of Lisa Steinberg, he says, the key factor was drugs—specifically, crack cocaine.

The Steinberg apartment was awash in drugs. And drugs, Stutman insists, explain what is too horrible to explain in any other way.

Joel Steinberg had been using drugs for many years. During those years, he had been getting steadily more abusive and physically violent. Finally, in the days leading up to his deadly attack on little Lisa, he had been smoking crack almost without pause.

The Steinberg case, says Stutman, was "a classic, textbook example of what happens to otherwise bright upper-middle-class people who start smoking cocaine, and how smoking cocaine so changes them emotionally and psychologically that over a period of time they beat a child to death."

Although the death of Lisa Steinberg received national attention, it was not an isolated tragedy. In January 1987, Darlwin Britt of Gary, Indiana, locked her nine-year-old daughter in an unheated apartment. The mother was so distracted by cocaine that she left the girl there for five days. By the time the little girl was finally released, her lower legs were severely frostbitten, and had to be amputated.

But no individual examples can indicate how widespread the problem is. Domestic violence and child neglect occur in millions of American homes. One million eight hundred thousand women are beaten by their husbands or lovers each year. Most of these women, like Hedda Nussbaum, stay with these men long after the first beating occurs. Approximately one out of every five women who needs emergency surgical help in American hospitals is suffering the effects of domestic violence.

Even more shocking, there are over 2.1 million reports of abused children each year. And child abuse seems to be getting worse. In New York City, for example, the number of battered children jumped almost 350 percent from 1986 to 1988. Over 1,200 American children die each year from the effects of neglect or beatings. And most of this violence is committed by the children's own fathers and mothers.

Drugs—including alcohol—play an important part in this epidemic of domestic violence. Many victims of abuse report that the abuser becomes a different person when on drugs or alcohol. Normally, some say, he or she is kind, and even gentle. But, when caught up in the chemical changes brought about by drugs, the person changes.

Drugs distort the user's sense of reality, often in unpredictable ways. They can dull the mind and emotions, making the user passive and indifferent. This can result in parents losing all sense of responsibility for their children. In extreme cases, parents cannot perform even the most basic tasks in caring for their children. They can forget to change a baby's diaper. They can ignore the fact that a child is engaging in dangerous behavior, like playing with matches or climbing out of windows. They can neglect to feed their children. They can even forget for days—and sometimes weeks—at a time that their children exist.

On the other hand, drugs can also intensify emotions and wipe away all self-restraint. Drugs can cause a parent to seethe with anger, or fly into a violent rage for no reason that anyone else can understand. An angry parent under the influence of a drug like crack cocaine can throw a child against a wall or out a window—or, like Joel Steinberg, beat a child to death with his or her bare hands.

According to *Newsweek* magazine, drugs or alcohol are involved in *at least* 40 percent of all cases of domestic abuse. But that figure is probably low, particularly when it comes to cases of extreme physical violence. According to Stutman, for example, 73 percent of the children like Lisa Steinberg, who are beaten to death in New York City, are children of substance abusers. And the drug most of them abuse is cocaine.

OVERLOADING THE CRIMINAL JUSTICE SYSTEM

Police are making more and more drug arrests every year. There has been a 76 percent increase in indictments for serious crimes in New York City over the past four years. Most of these crimes are drug-related. There are 2,000 police officers assigned full-time to drug offenses in the city, but they cannot handle the huge volume of cases they are called on to handle. Police in other cities are just as overworked.

The DEA does what it can to help, but both city and federal officials agree that it is pathetically understaffed at the local level. In Los Angeles, for example, the DEA had a total of 100 agents in 1989. That was no more than it had before Los Angeles became a major money laundering center, before drug-gang warfare sent the murder rate soaring, and before crack had even arrived in the United States. In 1989 there were a staggering 60,000 arrests for drug offenses in the city.

Our criminal justice system—the police, courts, and prisons—cannot handle the tidal wave of criminals being washed up by drugs. Some years ago, law-enforcement officials in Washington, D.C., carried out Operation Clean Sweep to rid the streets of drug dealers, at least temporarily. Altogether, some 16,000 people were arrested. But, as U.S. Attorney General

Richard Thornburgh has pointed out, only about 80 of them ever went to prison. In 1988 federal and state prosecutors in New York City won a total of 7,566 felony drug convictions. That number seems impressive, until it is compared to the 90,000 drug arrests in the city that year, 45,000 of which were for serious offenses. And those arrests, in turn, probably represented a small fraction of the serious drug crimes committed in the city that year.

New York and Washington, D.C., are typical of many other large cities around the country. There are simply not enough police officers to arrest the drug criminals. There are not enough prosecutors to prosecute them. There are not enough judges to hear the cases or enough courtrooms to hear them in. And, even if all the defendants could be brought to trial, there would not be enough defense attorneys to defend them.

But only a small number of these cases *are* brought to trial. In fact, most of them are not. Most drug cases are plea-bargained. This means that the prosecutors make a deal with the accused person. They agree to drop the most serious charges against the defendant, if he or she will plead guilty to a lesser crime.

Prosecutors plea-bargain for several reasons. Sometimes they don't have a very strong case, and they don't have the time or the staff to build a better one. What is more, they know that the judges are so busy that they don't have time to hear even the strong cases that they have. Plea-bargaining avoids the time and expense of a full trial.

As a practical matter, most drug offenders receive light sentences, often with little or no prison time at all. As DEA Agent Stutman explained to a Senate committee, many drug defendants get "two free bites of the apple." That is, they don't receive a stiff prison sentence until they are tried for their third offense. Out of the 90,000 people arrested for drug crimes in New York in 1988, said Stutman, only about 5,000 actually went to prison for a year or more. This reality, says Stutman, means that the threat of prison provides "no meaningful deterrent to drug traffickers."

Even so, our prisons are as overloaded as our courts. According to the government's General Accounting Office, the number of inmates in federal prisons doubled in the 1980s. As a result, by 1989, the prisons were operating at 56 percent over their capacity. And the situation is getting worse. According to the Department of Justice, there was a 7.3 percent rise in the number of prisoners in the nation's state and federal prisons in the first half of 1989. The way things are going, the prison population could double again by the year 2000.

According to Senator John Kerry of Massachusetts, when interviewed on the *MacNeil/Lehrer* television program, "Forty-five out of [the] fifty prison systems in the country are either under court order, or about to be under court order, because they're overcrowded." At some prisons, inmates have had to be released in droves. So many new prisoners were arriving to serve their sentences that there was no place to put them all.

CHAPTER SEVEN

THE PRICE
AMERICA PAYS
FOR DRUGS

IN the Old West, bandits waved guns in their victims' faces and demanded, "Your money or your life." Illegal drugs are worse than the old outlaws. They take both.

In this chapter we will examine some of the enormous losses American society suffers because of drugs. They are losses that cannot be counted in money alone. They must also be measured in terms of human suffering, wasted lives, early deaths, and social decay.

THE DRAIN ON THE ECONOMY

Drugs drain our economy of resources. Tens of billions of dollars are sent abroad each year to pay for the drugs Americans use. Those billions are lost to our society as surely as if some bandit had robbed us of them at gunpoint. It is money that cannot be spent in productive ways here in the United States. It is no longer available to the private sector to help build American industries and produce jobs for American workers. It is no longer available to the public sector to pay off the national debt or to rebuild the nation's aging roads, airports, and railroads. Nor is it available to feed the hungry or provide homes for the homeless.

As early as 1983 the U.S. Department of Health and Human Services was already estimating that drug abuse cost U.S. society $59 billion a year. The estimate included such expenses as treatment and support for addicts and victims, losses from drug-related thefts, and incarceration of drug criminals. It did not include the $100 to $200 billion that Americans pay for the drugs themselves.

WASTE IN THE WORKPLACE

When counting the price of drugs to our society, one cost that is sometimes forgotten is the loss of productivity from workers who use drugs. Drugs are used by people in every kind of job— from bank tellers to Wall Street financiers, and from assembly-line workers to university professors. In a recent poll, quoted by Senator Orrin Hatch of Utah, 49 percent of workers reported that drugs were being used by someone in their workplace. Thirty-two percent said that drugs of some kind were actually being sold there.

Drug use on the job wastes enormous amounts of time, talent, and resources. According to the National Institute on Drug Abuse, drug users are three times as likely to be late for work as nondrug users, and three and one-half times as likely to be involved in an accident on the job. They ask for sick leave, or time off, more than twice as often, and require three times as much in sick benefits as the average worker. In addition, they are five times as likely to file a complaint asking for workmen's compensation.

According to figures reported in *USA Today*, as much as 50 percent of the absenteeism in some companies is caused by drug problems. About 36 percent of all worker thefts are committed by drug users. What is more, approximately a third of all the defects in the quality of many companies' goods or services can be traced back to drugs.

In 1983 the U.S. Department of Health and Human Services estimated that such losses cost the American economy about $33,346,000,000 each year. But drugs in the workplace sometimes cost more than money. They cost human lives. Many drug-related on-the-job accidents are fatal, and some of them result in deaths to others besides the drug users themselves.

Drug use is most dangerous of all when it involves transportation workers. Truck drivers, bus drivers, train engineers, and even pilots have all been caught using drugs on the job. At least one air traffic controller at New York's JFK International Airport was found smoking crack during his work breaks.

THE CRISIS IN HEALTH CARE

Most drugs have undesirable physical and psychological side effects. These can range from drowsiness to a fatal heart attack, and from a sense of mild depression to a state of psychotic hysteria. When these effects are multiplied by the millions of drug abusers in the United States, they add up to a serious strain on the nation's health care system.

And the situation is getting worse. The National Institute on Drug Abuse recently surveyed hospital emergency rooms in 19 American cities. Of all the drugs, cocaine was causing the most medical emergencies in 17 of them. Hospitals in all but 3 of the cities reported record numbers of cocaine-related emergencies. Fourteen cities had record numbers of marijuana emergencies as well. And 11 of the 19 cities also reported record numbers of heroin emergencies.

But drug emergencies are only the tip of the iceberg. Over $2 billion was spent in 1983 just to provide treatment for drug addiction itself. Treatment for victims of drug-related crimes costs millions—and perhaps billions—of dollars more. Dr. Paul Goldstein of Narcotic and Drug Research, Inc., estimates that the victims of drug-related assaults alone require about $60 million in hospitalization expenses a year. And there is no way to tell how many cases of birth defects are caused by marijuana, or how many cases of advanced liver damage are caused by alcohol, and so on.

AIDS has been called the worst health care epidemic of the 20th century—perhaps of modern times. The intravenous use of drugs plays a major part in spreading this epidemic throughout American society. AIDS is spread by the mingling of blood or certain other bodily fluids. This can occur when two people use the same needle to inject drugs into their bloodstreams. In fact, shared needles are second only to sexual activity as a way of getting AIDS. Therefore, people who inject drugs are at an extremely high risk for contracting AIDS. And so are their spouses—and anyone else with whom they have sexual relations.

Ironically, just when fewer drug abusers are injecting heroin, more of them are beginning to inject cocaine. The effects of cocaine don't last nearly as long as the effects of heroin. This means that cocaine users tend to inject the drug more often, putting them at even higher risk than heroin users for contracting AIDS and other infectious diseases.

AIDS is not only a horrible disease for the person who has it, but it also causes severe mental and emotional suffering for all those who are close to the victim. It is also an extremely expensive disease, both for victims and for society at large. There is no cure for AIDS, and the few drugs that help at all are very expensive. Death from AIDS is often slow, and dying AIDS patients require a great deal of care.

According to statistics collected by the Department of Health and Human Services, the Centers for Disease Control, and others, about one-third of all AIDS victims in the United States are intravenous drug users. When the AIDS cases of spouses, lovers, and others who caught the disease from them are added in, it is likely that a much higher proportion of all AIDS cases in this country can be traced back to the abuse of drugs.

The millions of drug-related patients make it harder for other people to get prompt and effective medical care. Drug abusers and their victims fill many of the nation's emergency rooms. In some areas, they create waiting lists for desperately needed hospital beds. They assure that doctors, nurses, medical technologists, and other health care workers will be constantly overworked. At the very least, this reduces their efficiency and multiplies their mistakes.

All these extra strains add to America's already soaring medical costs. They put upward pressure on the prices charged for basic services and for medical insurance—even for those who are not themselves at high risk for AIDS and other drug-related diseases. They also increase the taxes everyone has to pay to support Medicaid and Medicare, the federal programs that provide medical attention for the poor and elderly.

THE CRACK BABIES

Perhaps the cruelest of all the medical consequences of drugs are their effects on the unborn children of drug-using mothers. Many of the children born with the HIV virus were infected by mothers who were themselves infected by dirty needles. Other children are born infected with various other diseases, with birth defects, or they are simply too weak to survive, all because their mother's health was destroyed by drugs before or during pregnancy.

About 375,000 babies are born each year to women who use drugs. Of these, as many as 300,000 are born addicted to the drugs their mothers used during pregnancy. Most are addicted to crack. Hundreds of millions of dollars worth of care is needed to nurse these babies until they are free of their addiction. Even then, as Mother Hale, a dedicated woman who devotes her life to the care of "drug babies," says, "These children will pay for this for the rest of their lives." For many the price will be paid not only in bad health, but in terrible emotional distress. James Hicks works with school-age children who were born to drug-using mothers. "These kids don't seem like they're dying," he says. "But emotionally, some are."

THE WAR FOR THE STREETS

We have already examined the influence of drugs on the soaring rates of violent crime. That crime has had a devastating effect on our nation's cities, where the bulk of America's hard-core drug addicts are located. (There are 76,000 known addicts in Washington, D.C., and over ten times that many in New York City.) As Mayor David Dinkins of New York City recently told a Senate committee, "Cities across America are under siege." There is "a real war on our streets," added Mayor Richard Berkley of Kansas City, Missouri. "A real war, in fact, *for* our streets."

Unfortunately, in some neighborhoods of many cities, the drug traffickers are winning that war. The law-abiding residents have surrendered. The streets belong to the pushers, the addicts, the prostitutes, and the street criminals scratching desperately for the money to buy drugs.

Drugs devastate neighborhoods, and eventually whole communities, in many different ways. First, of course, they damage people who live there and who consume the drugs themselves. They drain their users' financial and emotional resources. They make it hard for them to lead a normal life, to keep a job, or even to maintain a healthy relationship with their own families.

The public sale of drugs disrupts the community. It has been said that on many streets in New York City, the problem for police and customers alike isn't *finding* people who are selling drugs, but *avoiding* them. It is unpleasant, at best, to see the buying and selling of illegal drugs going on daily on the street outside your house. Considering how often turf wars and failed drug deals lead to violence, it can also be extremely dangerous.

NEW YORK POST

Thursday July 31 1986   40 cents beyond 50-mile zone, except L.I.   **35 CENTS**

SPECIAL REPORT **Drug crisis in N.Y.**

GIVE US BACK OUR CITY!

POST EDITORIAL

THE people of New York have had it.

From the Coney Island boardwalk to the bustling sidewalks of Wall Street, from the Queensborough Public Library in Flushing to the schoolyards of Washington Heights, the drug epidemic is everywhere — threatening to rip apart the fabric of this city.

And from these same places, New Yorkers are crying out — in fear, but also in anger.

Their message is plain: "Give us back our city!"

For all the Operation Pressure Points and all the special crack units, the enemy is gaining territory — at a rapid pace.

To say "This is war" is no exaggeration.

Indeed, New York is at the threshold of an urban guerrilla war, as honest citizens fight to reclaim their city, block by block, schoolyard by school-

Continued on Page 34

ENOUGH IS ENOUGH!

The big crack crunch is on
PAGES 4 & 5

Readers want fast action
PAGES 34 & 43

In 1986, the front page of the *New York Post* newspaper reflected the public's anger and frustration over the problem of illegal drugs.

Drugs breed fear, not just in those who use them, but in everyone around them as well. Eventually, when drug abuse and the resulting crime get bad enough, people begin to leave. Those who can afford to do so move out. They flee to another neighborhood where drug use is less prevalent, or to another city altogether. The only people who stay are the drug abusers, the criminals who prey on them, and those honest residents who are too poor to get out. When this happens, the war for the streets has been won—by the drug traffickers.

RAISING RACIAL TENSIONS

Drugs may be the most urgent short-term crisis facing America today. But many social scientists would argue that the country's most serious long-term problem is racism. And drugs make that problem worse. Many people in both the white and black communities are blaming each other for the drug problem.

Many white people think of drugs, and the violence that goes with them, as primarily a black problem. They see that it is in the inner city that drug dealing is most open and drug violence most extreme. And the inner city is mostly black. So are the drug-dealing gangs that white people see on television. As a result, many whites come to identify black people with drug criminals, and to regard drugs as a problem that is reaching out from the inner cities to ensnare their children.

As a matter of fact, a higher percentage of white people than black people use drugs. According to a study conducted by the National Institute on Drug Abuse, 25 percent of all white 12- to 17-year-olds have used an illegal drug in the past year, compared to only 19 percent of blacks. Among 18- to 25-year-olds, about 18 percent of whites used cocaine last year, compared to only 11 percent of blacks. Under these conditions, as Hubert Williams, the head of the Police Foundation, has said, "To think of this problem as a minority problem, as a black problem, is ludicrous." And yet many people, both white and black, do think of it that way.

The black people who think of drugs as a black problem tend to see it as a problem imposed on them by white people. After all, most of the honest citizens who are forced to live in the worst inner-city neighborhoods are black. They are the ones who suffer most from the destruction wreaked by drugs. Trapped in devastated neighborhoods, they experience the violence and fear around them. They watch many of their young men being destroyed by drugs, while others are shot down in the streets. And they are left to search for reasons. Why? they ask. Why is it blacks who suffer the most terrible effects of illegal drugs?

Having suffered through generations of discrimination, it is easy for many black people to see drugs as another product of white racism. They remember that heroin was first brought into the black community by white people. (The Mafia, which controlled the heroin traffic for so long, was white.)

Even today, they reason, although the street pusher is often black, the drug lords behind him are usually white. The Mafia is still white. The leaders of the drug cartels are white—at least, they're not black. Many blacks suspect that white people have brought drugs into their neighborhoods for two reasons. First, to take away their money. And second, to destroy the black community altogether. Some black leaders have even suggested that drugs are a kind of genocide—a plague, brought on them by whites, that threatens to wipe out their whole race.

CORRUPTION

"Corruption" means rot. It is a form of decay that breaks down the structure of whatever it attacks. It is the process that turns food into garbage, and healthy tissue into disease. When applied to living things, it is associated with death. Drugs spread corruption wherever they are found.

Addiction to drugs corrupts the people who use them. It makes them willing to do anything for drugs, no matter how illegal or immoral. Addicts will lie, cheat, become prostitutes, steal, and even murder to get drugs. But just as the chemicals themselves corrupt the people who use them, the dishonest money that surrounds illegal drugs corrupts society as a whole.

The corrupting effects of drug money are felt almost everywhere, especially in some of the poor countries that supply the raw materials of drugs. In such countries, as Ambassador Carlos

Delius of Bolivia has said, "drugs have corrupted government officials, the police and army. The amount of those dollars floating around is just too great a temptation for people who barely earn enough...to survive."

Even in the United States, many poor people turn to drug dealing as a way of getting the money they cannot earn in any other way. But there are also many prosperous people throughout our society who willingly accept indirect profits from drug money.

Some of the most obvious are the lawyers who work for druglords. There is certainly nothing wrong with a lawyer defending someone charged with a drug crime; in fact, our legal system *requires* all defendants to be represented. But some lawyers go far beyond defending individual clients. They build their whole careers by erecting legal walls behind which drug kingpins can continue to carry on their immoral and illegal trade.

These lawyers make a deliberate choice to serve the interests of drug traffickers. That is a legal choice to make. It can also be an extremely profitable one. But there are many people, both inside and outside the legal profession, who believe it is an immoral choice. And the reason most of these lawyers make it is greed. In the view of Geoffrey Hazard, an expert in the study of ethics and the law, "The legal profession is being corrupted" by this greed.

Lawyers are hardly the only ones who reap indirect profits from drugs. In some neighborhoods, it is common for young people to pay cash for expensive cars. The dealers who sell them these cars know very well that the money they are taking comes from the sale of drugs. Respectable real estate agents pocket large commissions for finding mansions for drug kingpins. Boat dealers make big profits selling yachts to drug traffickers— boats they can reasonably assume will be used to smuggle drugs. It may not be illegal to sell expensive items to drug criminals, but it is a form of corruption. It means cooperating with the drug dealers, and it means profiting from the sale of drugs.

A more direct form of profiting from the drug business is the sale of so-called precursor chemicals. These are the chemicals used in the manufacture of cocaine and other drugs. Most of these chemicals are made by respectable American pharmaceutical (drug) companies and then sold to "front" companies in Colombia and elsewhere. The American companies argue that these chemicals can be used for various purposes. They don't *know* when they sell them that the customers plan to use them to make illegal drugs. But, government authorities in Colombia and elsewhere complain, the companies don't try to find out either. They would rather take the substantial profits they make from selling to the drug traffickers, and look the other way.

Another form of corruption is demonstrated by the police and other public officials who take drugs themselves. Unfortunately, this is not a rare occurrence. Many government officials, at almost every level of government, have been caught using drugs.

Police are among the most frequent offenders. In New York City alone, hundreds of police officers were caught using cocaine in 1988. Shockingly, although 300 of them were suspended for short periods of time, most of them were not even dismissed from the police force.

Very often, corrupt police officers are found among those specifically assigned to antidrug operations. (This is probably because they are the ones who are subject to the most temptation.) Sometimes they are not only guilty of *using* the drugs themselves but they occasionally cross the line into *dealing* in illegal drugs.

Large amounts of drugs have sometimes disappeared after they have been taken into custody by the police. In some cases, they have simply been misplaced. But in other cases, they have been stolen by members of the police force, then sold back to drug traffickers to sell on the streets. A major case of this kind of corruption is the subject of an excellent and exciting book, *Prince of the City*, by Robert Daley.

In 1989 federal DEA agents arrested four of their own officers on drug charges. The highest ranking of the four was Edward O'Brien, who had once been in charge of the DEA's office in Springfield, Massachusetts. He was arrested while transporting

62 pounds of cocaine from Miami to Boston, in order to sell it to an undercover agent he believed to be a drug trafficker.

These are not just examples of hypocrisy, of people saying one thing and doing another. These are examples of the most basic kind of official corruption—a rotting process that strikes at the very structure of trust between the people and their government. By dealing with the drug dealers, police and other officials violate their oaths of office and betray their public duty. Instead of protecting society against the drug criminals, they have become drug criminals themselves.

THE TOLL ON THE CHILDREN

Perhaps the highest price society pays for drugs is the toll they take on children. Drugs corrupt families as surely as they corrupt other institutions. Millions of children are being raised in families where at least one parent is abusing drugs. In far too many cases, both parents are. This is true of children of all races and all economic classes. Tragically for everyone, few abusers of any social or economic class make good parents. We have already seen the effects of drug abuse on family violence. But drugs also have other, almost equally destructive, effects.

At best, drug abuse interferes with a healthy family life. At worst, it destroys it. Drug abuse breaks down the bonds of trust and affection that should exist between family members. It contributes to economic problems and the resulting tensions in the home.

Drug abuse tears families apart. It leads addicts to desert the spouses and children they no longer care about as much as they care about their drugs. And it causes spouses and children to leave home, in order to avoid the pain of dealing with someone hopelessly addicted to a destructive drug. More than 120,000 children are arrested for running away from home each year. They are only a fraction of the total number of runaways. Many of these children come from drug-plagued families. By the time they are arrested, many of them have become involved in drugs themselves.

The devastating effects of drugs on family life are being made worse by the growing "femalization" of the drug problem. Until recently, most heroin and other hard-drug addicts were male. This was bad enough for those children whose addicted fathers lost their jobs, beat them, deserted their families, or died from an overdose of drugs. But at least there was usually a mother in the home to care for them and to give them emotional support.

But the newer drugs are equal opportunity poisons. According to Robert Stutman of the DEA, at least 50 percent of today's cocaine and crack addicts are female. Many of them are mothers—often single mothers who are solely responsible for raising their children.

Mothers caught up in heavy cocaine and crack abuse can become zombies. The drug, and their own hunger for it, makes them incapable of satisfying their own physical and emotional needs. They are even less able to satisfy the needs of their children. Some cannot provide their children with food and clothing, much less with emotional comfort and moral guidance.

Ironically, when drugs destroy families, they also destroy the best defense society has against drugs. As the U.S. government's "drug czar" William Bennett told a meeting of the Congressional Black Caucus, "You give me back the nuclear family...and I [sic] give you a 75% to 80% reduction in the drug problem."

In many big city neighborhoods, even the children whose own families are free of drug abuse have to live with it every day. They have to pass by drug dealers on their way to and from grade school. They find themselves stepping over unconscious— if not dead—drug addicts on the stairs of their apartment buildings. They live with the fear of being trapped in the crossfire of drug-related violence at any time.

In conditions like these, it is hardly surprising that so many young people are caught up in the world of drugs. It is not at all unusual for high school students, white and black, to deal in drugs. Fifteen- and 16-year-old dealers have taken to carrying beepers, like those used by doctors, to connect them to their suppliers. Schools in some cities have banned beepers because their noise was disrupting classes. In Philadelphia it is reported that children as young as eight are being enlisted as messengers for older drug dealers.

CHAPTER EIGHT

PLANS FOR
THE WAR
ON DRUGS

RICHARD Nixon's measures against heroin were the first "war on drugs." His successors, Presidents Ford and Carter, took no dramatic new steps to attack drugs. By the time Ronald Reagan was elected president in 1980, both drug use and drug-related crime were on the rise. Drugs were becoming a hot political issue. Before long, another "war" was declared.

REAGAN'S WAR

The main enemy in President Reagan's war against drugs was cocaine, not heroin. And, although the president spoke out strongly against drugs, he did not want to spend a lot of government money fighting them. As a result, his "war" was not waged very aggressively.

Nevertheless, there were two well-publicized fronts in the Reagan drug war. One was aimed at shutting off the supply of the drug. The other was designed to reduce the demand for drugs. The first was led by Vice-President George Bush, who headed the National Narcotics Border Interdiction System (NNBIS). Its job was to interdict (or stop) the smuggling of drugs into the country.

Even before the NNBIS, Vice-President Bush had headed the federal South Florida Task Force, a law-enforcement unit with the job of interdicting the flow of drugs onto Florida. It was made up of agents from several federal agencies, including the DEA and the Coast Guard. However, it was not given any new money to work with. It had to operate on money from the agencies' regular budgets.

The biggest success on the interdiction front was the effort to shut off the flow of drugs onto Florida's southern coast. At that time Miami was the cocaine capital of the United States. Incredible amounts of the drug were flooding through the city. There was so much drug money coming in that it was fueling an economic boom in the entire Miami area.

The government's effort to choke off the supply of cocaine into South Florida was successful. Miami quickly lost its reputation as the center of the cocaine trade. But the NNBIS was not nearly so successful elsewhere, particularly along the immense and mostly unprotected border with Mexico. The drug lords simply rerouted the cocaine that had been coming in by way of Florida, sending it through Mexico instead.

The other front in President Reagan's war on drugs was led by his wife, Nancy. It was an effort to persuade young people to "Just say no!" to drugs. That slogan was featured on a torrent of billboards, advertisements, and public-service TV spots. Mrs. Reagan traveled around the country herself, speaking in schools and hammering the message home—don't use drugs.

Many people scoffed at the First Lady's campaign. They complained that it was shallow and even a little silly. They insisted that drug abuse was too complicated a problem to be

Young people marched at an antidrug rally in Austin, Texas, supporting Nancy Reagan's campaign to "Just Say No!" to drugs.

more cocaine was coming into the country than ever before. Worse, the street price of cocaine had dropped by 75 percent, making it that much easier for abusers to afford.

PRESIDENT BUSH TAKES OVER

When George Bush accepted the Republican nomination for president, he made a dramatic promise to the nation's drug dealers. "Your day is over," he told them. "You are history!" At his inauguration, in January 1989, he made an equally determined pledge to the people of the United States. "Take my word for it," he declared. "This scourge [of drugs] will stop."

But the new president's actual plan for fighting the drug war came as a disappointment to many people. To them the new president's plan looked very much like the old president's plan.

attacked by simple-minded slogans. There was no way, they said, that the legions of street addicts would stop snorting cocaine and smoking crack merely because the First Lady told them to "just say no."

But Mrs. Reagan's campaign was not aimed at the street addicts. It was aimed at the tens of millions of young Americans who were not yet using drugs: kids who were tempted to experiment with them, and who might be persuaded by the idea that "everybody else is doing it." And, in that respect, it may have succeeded—at least partially. It is hard to tell how much influence it actually had. But the number of new young drug abusers did fall dramatically in the late 1980s. And that was the group the First Lady's campaign was designed to reach.

Meanwhile, the rest of the drug war was failing to shut off the flow of drugs into the country—even after Congress forced the president to spend more money. In September 1988 Congress passed a massive antidrug bill. It made drugs a national priority by setting up a new cabinet level department, the National Office of Drug Control Policy. Its director became known as the nation's drug czar.

The bill gave the military new powers to interdict drugs, and law-enforcement authorities new weapons to use in prosecuting suspected drug criminals. In addition, it set up a variety of antidrug programs. They ranged from greater federal help for law enforcement, to new efforts to warn people about the dangers of drugs, to better treatment programs to help addicts who wanted to conquer their addictions. (Money for treatment had actually gone *down* sharply in the mid-1980s.)

Most importantly, the bill backed up the new assault on drugs with funds—$6 billion to be spent fighting drugs over the next three years. President Reagan was reluctant to spend that much money. But, with national concern about drugs on the increase, he signed the bill in November.

None of this seemed to help, at least on the supply side. George Bush succeeded Ronald Reagan as president in 1989. By the time he laid out plans for his own drug war that September,

The main difference was that it called for more money—$7.9 billion in the first full year. But critics of the plan quickly pointed out that less than $1 billion of this was new money. The rest had already been authorized by Congress. And when Congress eventually passed the war-on-drugs bill, it added over $1 billion to what the president had requested.

The next January, President Bush unveiled a somewhat broader antidrug strategy for 1991 and beyond. The key to the new plan was an effort to attack drugs on every possible front. As drug czar William Bennett explained, it was intended to be "a comprehensive effort, putting pressure on every point of the spectrum."

But, once again, critics argued that it was not nearly ambitious enough to do the job. Critics like Mathea Falco, a former assistant secretary of state for International Narcotics, complained that it was simply more of the Reagan strategy: tough talk but little money to back it up with action. The president talked about waging a massive war on drugs, but he was only asking for $10.6 billion to fight it. That wasn't much money to fight a war, particularly considering the size and power of the enemy. Cocaine worth almost twice that much had been seized in a single raid in September 1989. Among the critics was Governor Mario Cuomo of New York, who declared that "Every governor, every mayor knows that this is a pittance that they're putting into drugs."

Despite the criticism of President Bush's plan, it is likely that it will provide the blueprint for the government's drug war for the rest of the 1990s. In the remainder of this chapter, we will examine the president's strategy for the drug war, and the controversies that surround it.

The debate over antidrug strategy reflects a basic difference in philosophy. One side sees drugs as essentially a law-enforcement problem. The other sees them primarily as a symptom of deeper and even more serious social ills. The first side tends to favor "get tough" measures designed to stamp out the supply of drugs. The second side favors measures to attack the social and economic problems it believes underlie the demand for drugs.

EDUCATION AND TREATMENT

Two key elements in fighting demand for drugs are education and treatment. Education includes both antidrug campaigns like Mrs. Reagan's "Just Say No!" and programs for drug education in the schools. Treatment emphasizes both medical and psychological help for addicts trying to conquer their addictions. These kinds of programs are particularly important to those who view drugs as a reflection of even deeper social problems. As Mayor David Dinkins of New York City testified to Congress, such people are convinced that "treatment and education are the way to go." President Bush's 1990 plan called for moderate increases in both areas.

Altogether, the plan sets aside $1.2 billion for education. At a Senate Judiciary Committee hearing on the president's plan, Senator Joseph Biden of Delaware complained that under the proposal, only about 40 percent of the nation's schoolchildren would receive "anything resembling" drug education. Drug czar Bennett responded that he did "not believe you can inoculate children against drug abuse [by educating them]. I know children." Bennett was not arguing against drug education. He is, in fact, in favor of it. But it still seems to some observers, including Elias J. Duryea, a health education expert from the University of New Mexico, a shocking statement for him to make. Duryea argues that studies prove that education can, in fact, "inoculate" young people against drug abuse. Dr. Bennett, however, would clearly put the government's priorities—and most of its antidrug money—elsewhere.

The Bush plan also calls for another $1.5 billion to be set aside for improving federal and state treatment facilities. A major element of this part of the plan calls for an overhaul of the nation's existing treatment centers. The majority of them were established to deal with heroin addicts, but most of the people now seeking treatment are addicted to cocaine.

Most experts believe that about 25 percent of drug addicts are so hooked that they will not be able to break their habit under any circumstances. Another 25 percent will be able to stop on their own. The remaining 50 percent could benefit from treatment.

According to William Bennett, the Bush plan means that 1.7 million addicts will be treated each year. But some critics, including Senator Ted Kennedy of Massachusetts, point out that this is nowhere near the 3 million drug abusers who desperately need treatment.

DRUG TESTING

Traces of all three of the most-abused drugs remain in the body for a long time after the drugs are taken. One way to find out if someone has been using drugs is to test the person's urine, blood, or hair for these substances. Drug testing is becoming an increasingly important weapon in the drug war. The Bush administration has ordered the workers in three major industries to be tested for drug use. They are the transportation, defense, and nuclear industries—all fields that have a direct effect on public safety.

In addition, the Bush administration has moved to make testing easier for businesses and other institutions in the private sector. Some government contracts now require businesses that provide goods or services to the government to test their employees for drugs.

The use of drug tests is growing in private industry, even in companies that don't do business with the government. According to the Bureau of Labor Statistics, about 3.2 percent of all private companies were already testing their employees by the end of 1989.

Proponents of on-the-job testing argue that it is useful for several reasons. It cuts down on accidents by removing drug abusers from situations where they could put themselves or others in danger. By uncovering drug users, it allows companies to direct them to drug counseling or more elaborate forms of treatment. For businesses, testing is an economic measure. As we have already seen, employees who use drugs cost their employers money. Senator Orrin Hatch reported that one company in his home state of Utah saved $1 million in its first year of drug testing.

Professional sports leagues, including the National Basketball Association and the National Football League, have led the way in drug testing. In general, when one of their athletes tests positive for drugs, he is ordered to receive treatment. If he tests positive a second (or third) time, he is banned from the sport, either for a certain period or for life. The United States Navy has a similar policy for its members.

But many people oppose widespread drug testing. They complain that drug tests are sometimes inaccurate. Even more fundamentally, they argue that tesing violates individual rights. It requires people to provide physical evidence against themselves and invades their privacy. Being made to urinate into a bottle (often in front of a stranger who is watching to make sure you don't cheat on the test) can be humiliating. What is more, they say, most businesses do not use the tests to help employees and job applicants. Instead of sending them for help, they simply fire them or deny them a job in the first place.

Some educators want drug testing to be used in the nation's schools. They argue that it is necessary to find young drug users and turn them off drugs as soon as possible. As the 1990s begin, however, the law still forbids the testing of most students in the public schools. Exceptions have been made in respect to certain kinds of students, including those who play varsity sports. The same laws do not apply to private schools, whether religious or otherwise. In January 1990 Saint Sabrina, a Roman Catholic school on the South Side of Chicago, became the first grade school in the country to start random drug testing for students.

Opponents of school testing make many of the same arguments opponents of other kinds of testing make. They maintain that it is just as wrong to violate a student's rights as it is to violate the rights of an employee. Ironically, in a recent survey of high school students, the majority of them supported the idea of drug testing in schools—even though most of them agreed that it would be a violation of their own rights. And 62 percent of

Wisconsin residents polled by the Gordon S. Black Corporation favored uniform testing of all high school students at the beginning of the school year.

Some who oppose testing see polls like this one as signs that the drug war has gone too far. They argue that the nation is overreacting to the drug problem. They warn that we must be careful not to sacrifice our personal liberties in the fight against drugs.

ERADICATION

In the debate over antidrug strategy, the Bush administration clearly comes down on the side of those who see drug abuse as primarily a law-enforcement problem. The main thrust of its attack on drugs is aimed at the supply.

That attack begins with an effort to eradicate (or destroy) the crops that are the raw material of the big three drugs. In the United States itself, $35 million is slated for an effort to eradicate the homegrown cannabis crop. Abroad, the emphasis will be on coca.

Eradication of coca is a key aim of a series of foreign policy measures known as the Andean Initiative. Several methods have been suggested for attacking the coca crop. They range from spraying the plants with herbicides to infesting them with a special kind of caterpillar that might gobble up their leaves before the coca could be harvested. Some naturalists object to such plans on the grounds that they are dangerous to the environment. Herbicides could poison nearby water supplies, and caterpillars that eat coca leaves would eat other leaves as well. If they got out of control, they might strip the forests of the whole region.

Eradication is controversial for other reasons as well, both in the Andean countries and in the United States. One important element in Bush's proposal is the allocation of $2.2 billion to be sent to Peru, Bolivia, and Colombia over the next five years. Some of that money would be spent to help the governments fight the drug traffickers. The rest would go to help the Andean economies adjust to the loss of the money that now comes in as a result of the coca crop.

Financial help will be desperately needed by the Peruvian and Bolivian farmers who now support themselves growing coca. Andean authorities point out that these farmers have to do something to keep themselves and their families alive. If coca is not replaced by something at least as profitable, the farmers will do one of two things. They will starve or they will join the left-wing guerrillas who area already fighting against the Andean governments. Andean leaders are not willing to sentence their own famers to starvation, nor do they want them to take up arms against the government.

But, the Andean authorities argue, the $2.2 billion being offered them is nowhere near enough to make up the enormous losses their economies would suffer from destruction of the coca crop. According to Peru's ambassador to the United States, for example, coca brings between $754 million and $954 million to Peru's economy every year. Total eradication would mean a loss of over $3.5 billion to Peru alone over five years. And that doesn't even take into account the losses that would be suffered by Bolivia and Colombia.

On the other hand, some members of Congress object to sending the Andean farmers any money at all. That, they say, would be "paying people not to break the law."

Other critics of the eradication/aid plan doubt that it can be effective in the long run. They point to recent history to make their case. Just a few years ago, Bolivian coca farmers were paid $2,000 per hectare (about 2.5 acres) to destroy their crops. The program lasted for three years. After it was over, they still had no other way of making a living. So they used what was left of the money to plant more coca. In the end, almost twice as many hectares were planted with coca than before the eradication program began.

Even if the coca crops in the Andean countries could be wiped out, that wouldn't stop people from planting coca elsewhere. There are several other places in the world that could grow coca, including Brazil—a country so large that policing it to prevent the growing of coca would be impossible.

EXTRADITION

Another key element of the U.S.'s Andean strategy is the extradition of drug criminals to the United States—that is, having drug traffickers captured in Andean countries brought to the United States for trial. Most of the extraditions so far have been from Colombia.

In Colombia the drug war is a real, shooting war. In August 1989 killers working for one of the cartels assassinated an anticartel presidential candidate, Luis Carlos Galan, at a political rally. From that time on, the government and the cartels have been engaged in a bloody and desperate battle. Over the next four months, the cartels killed 187 government officials and civilians. According to *Time* magazine, they carried out 250 bombings during the same period. Even before this latest outburst of violence, about 50 judges and 150 other court employees had already been murdered in Colombia.

The best-known victim on the other side was Jose Gonzales Rodriguez Gacha, known as one of the most vicious leaders of the Medillin cartel. He was killed in a gun battle with Colombian forces just before Christmas, 1989.

Because of the widespread intimidation of Colombian courts, the government of President Virgilio Barco favors extradition. By January 1990 nine cartel figures had been sent to the United States. The highest-ranking was Carlos Lehder, one of the most colorful of the Medillin leaders, who is now serving a long sentence in a U.S. prison for smuggling three tons of cocaine.

The drug lords are apparently so frightened of extradition that they have launched a campaign of terror to force the government to change its policy. Whenever they set off a bomb in downtown Bogotá, or murder a judge, or blow up an airplane, they claim responsibility in the name of the "Extraditables." Some cartel leaders have even offered peace in the drug war in return for an end to extradition. A recent poll showed that most Colombians believe that would be a good deal for the government to make. So far, however, Barco has refused to compromise. He doesn't trust the cartels to keep their promise. And, besides, he feels that Colombia has sacrificed too much to give up now. Speaking before a Senate committee in early 1990, Colombia's ambassador to the United States, Victor Mosquera-Chaux, pledged that his government would bring the drug lords to justice.

In any case, extradition has so far done little to stop the flow of cocaine from Colombia to the United States. As Rafael Santos, a Colombian journalist, commented on the ABC television program *Nightline*, "Every time you extradite a Colombian, 20 tons of cocaine show up on the streets of Los Angeles." And meanwhile, Colombia itself remains awash in a bloodbath of murder and terror.

THE INVASION OF PANAMA

The biggest battle yet in the drug war took place in Panama. Shortly before Christmas, 1989, a U.S. invasion force landed in that small Central American country. They had come to remove General Manuel Noriega from power and to return him to the United States for trial. Noriega had been indicted in two Florida courts for helping the Colombian cartels move drugs and drug money through Panama to the United States.

The United States had asked Panama to extradite him, but Panama had refused. This was not surprising. Although Noriega was not the president of Panama, he was its ruler. He ran the government from his position as head of the armed forces. Months earlier, an election had threatened to give Panama's presidency to an anti-Noriega candidate. The general had used his control of the military to cancel the election before the votes could be counted. In addition to capturing Noriega, the invasion was designed to put in power the candidate the United States believed would have won the election.

After only a few days of fighting, the American forces gained control of Panama. Noriega himself escaped capture for some time by taking refuge in the residence of the Vatican's diplomatic representative in Panama. Eventually, however, Noriega surrendered and was flown to Miami, which he was imprisoned while awaiting trial.

In the aftermath of the invasion, most Americans, and most Panamanians, approved of the U.S. action. They considered it both a step toward democracy in Panama and a major victory in the war against the international drug trade. But a minority of people in both countries—along with almost all the governments of Latin America—condemned the invasion.

Few of the critics defended Manuel Noriega. But they strongly objected to what the United States had done to unseat him. They argued that the United States had no right to indict a foreign leader and then invade his country to capture him. How would the United States feel if Iran indicted President Bush for some imagined crime, and then sent soldiers to kidnap *him?*

Some critics also accused the United States of hypocrisy. The CIA had been friendly with Noriega for many years before the 1989 invasion. As Frederick Kempe explains in his book, *Divorcing the Dictator,* the Reagan administration had used Noriega to help the Contra rebels who were fighting the left-wing government of Nicaragua. More than once, the general had had dinner at the private home of Reagan's director of the CIA, William Casey. And all this time the U.S. government had known about Noriega's drug dealings. It had even helped him to conceal them.

According to some, the government's hypocrisy went even deeper than its long, friendly relationship with Noriega. According to Ramon Millan-Rodriguez, the captured money launderer for the Medillin cartel, an agent working for the U.S. government had approached him to contribute money to the Contras. And, Millan claims, between $9 and $10 million of the cartel's money was actually given to the Contras—at the U.S. government's request!

DOMESTIC LAW ENFORCEMENT

As a part of the Andean Initiative $206 million will go to Colombia, Peru, and Bolivia to help their police and military forces combat drug criminals. But the real heart of the Bush strategy is law enforcement here in the United States.

Altogether, the plan calls for $4.3 billion to go to federal and state law enforcement. A new National Drug Intelligence Center will be established to keep track of drug crimes—and drug criminals—across the country. The bulk of the money will be divided between direct federal spending and grants to state and local governments. It will provide more prosecutors, as well as 6,000 new spaces in the nation's prisons to house the drug criminals they will presumably convict.

The military budget will get another $1.2 billion to expand the military's role in the drug war. The antidrug role of the U.S. Customs Office will also be expanded. John Heinrich of the U.S. Customs Service, for one, welcomes the increased help of the military along the nation's borders. But others object to using the military in this way. Among them is retired U.S. Admiral Gene La Rocque, currently of the Center for Defense Information. Speaking at a televised press conference criticizing the president's 1990 plan, La Rocque insisted that "The military is entirely unsuited for the drug war...It's a blunt instrument," he argued, "not a police force."

The plan calls for new penalties for some drug-related crimes. The death penalty, in particular, is to be used more often. Even before the Bush plan was announced, there was a federal law allowing the death penalty for "drug kingpins." But the 1990 proposals would apply it to a whole new range of drug offenses, including supplying drugs to pregnant women or to people who would be "likely" to die from using them. William Bennett and other administration spokespersons argue that broader use of the death penalty will deter (or discourage) drug dealers. Besides, they insist, it is *just*. Speaking about those who might be executed under the proposal, Bennett declared that "the penalty of death is what they deserve."

But critics argue that the death penalty is unlikely to be an effective deterrent to drug traffickers. One of these critics is Representative John Conyers of Michigan. Interviewed on the C-SPAN cable television network early in 1990, he asked, "What could make someone think [that] people who impose the death penalty on each other on a daily basis could possible be deterred by us imposing the death penalty on them?"

Besides, critics protest, constitutional safeguards make it difficult to impose the death penalty on anyone—even mass murderers and political assassins. If prosecutors try to impose it on a whole new class of drug criminals, they argue, it will only lead to endless appeals and clog up the nation's courts even more than they are already.

Another part of Bush's strategy involves the Financial Crimes Enforcement Network (FINCEN), whose job it is to track down and seize drug traffickers' property. Even before the 1990 plan was announced, $15 million was being spent to "follow the money." Millions of dollars worth of yachts, automobiles, and even houses belonging to suspected drug dealers had already been seized in the FINCEN effort.

There is also an important international side to the search for drug money. In 1989 Colombian officials raided the estates of a number of drug lords. Among the papers they found was "a long list" of bank accounts owned by the cartels and their leaders in both American and foreign banks. In November 1989 the DEA announced that at least $60 million belonging to Jose Gonzales Rodriguez Gacha had been frozen in banks in five different countries. A month later the fugitive Gacha was shot down by Colombian authorities.

The Bush plan has set aside $46 million especially for law enforcement in five "high intensity drug areas." These are Houston, Los Angeles, Miami, New York, and the entire southwest border with Mexico. The five areas were chosen because each is a center for the importation and distribution of drugs throughout the United States. Success in the battle against drugs in these areas, the administration believes, would help the entire country. The new money is specifically targeted to provide these areas with more drug agents and prosecutors.

Local officials in the five areas welcome the help. But some of them feel that it is too little to do much good. Others think the money should go directly to the local governments, instead of to federal agents and prosecutors. Still others complain that simply convicting more criminals will do little good. New ones will soon take their place.

LOOKING TO THE FUTURE

Strom Thurmond, a powerful "get tough" senator from South Carolina, hailed President Bush's 1990 proposals as "a solid, well thought out plan for action." Supporters like Senator Thurmond praised the plan for its emphasis on law enforcement and cutting back on the supply of drugs.

Critics, meanwhile, protested that it failed to address the deeper social and economic issues they saw as underlying the demand for drugs—issues such as poverty, racial tension, homelessness, unemployment, and the need for job training. New York City government official Eleanor Holmes Norton commented that "the War on Drugs is great at taking prisoners." But, she added, "It is terrible at treating the wounded."

In any case, government strategy in the 1990s is likely to remain similar to what it was in the 1980s. It could be called a "little-more-of-the-same strategy." It provides for a little more treatment and education on the one hand, and a little more law enforcement on the other. In that sense, it is a compromise between the two opposing points of view about the drug problem. But it is a compromise that is heavily weighted toward the law-and-order side.

CHAPTER NINE

CAN

THE DRUG WAR

EVER END?

THERE is no hope that today's drug war—or anything like it—will put an end to drug abuse in America. Even the drug war's strongest supporters don't argue that it will be won in any final sense. The only real hope is that it may succeed in bringing drug abuse under some sort of control. This may mean that drug abuse will be confined to a smaller segment of the population, or reduced to a level where it will no longer be a major national concern.

Even if the drug war succeeds to that extent, it can never really end. There will always be a need for measures to educate the young about the dangers of drugs, to treat addicts, and to combat the drug dealers who prey on both groups. Anyone looking for a real end to the drug war has to look for more extreme solutions.

Speaking on the ABC television program *Nightline,* in September 1989, Pat Buchanan, the commentator and one-time adviser to President Nixon, named the stark alternatives. "There are two ways you can end this war. One is legalize [drugs] and get the crime out of it. The other is...the 'Malaysian solution.'"

In this concluding chapter, we will examine these two extreme proposals for ending the war on drugs once and for all.

THE "MALAYSIAN SOLUTION"

What Buchanan calls the "Malaysian solution" is the get-tough strategy carried to its farthest limits. In the Southeast Asian nation of Malaysia, the punishment for the possession of illegal drugs is death. It is as simple—and as brutal—as that.

Whether the culprit is a native or a foreigner, a simple user or a major drug trafficker, the law is applied without exception. Even naive tourists from the United States have been arrested, tried, and executed for bringing small amounts of drugs into Malaysia for their own use. Not surprisingly, Malaysia does not have a serious drug problem. It is unlikely that the United States would have a drug problem either if it adopted the Malaysian law as its own.

But, as Buchanan pointed out, "this country is not going to go that far." Most Americans are simply not willing to be that sweeping and merciless. And even if they were, there would be little likelihood that such an extensively applied death penalty would be accepted as constitutional by the United States Supreme Court. It would probably be ruled out as "cruel and unusual punishment."

But anything less is unlikely to do the job. In recent years, laws have been passed by both the federal government and some states that impose longer sentences for drug crimes. In some states, drug dealers with a certain number of convictions are sent to prison for life without chance of parole.

But there is little, if any, evidence that these harsher penalties have reduced the sale or use of drugs. In fact, some opponents of such measures argue that they have only resulted in younger and younger children being pressed into drug dealing. Dealers who worry about being caught don't get out of the drug business. Instead, they hire young children to sell their drugs for them— children who are not subject to the same extreme sentences because of their age.

Even if twice as many drug dealers could be arrested, and twice as many prisons could be built to hold them, it might make little difference. As New York District Court Judge Robert Sweet has pointed out, the United States already puts more of its people in jail than any country in the developed world except South Africa. And yet we have one of the worst drug problems—if not *the* worst—in the world.

LEGALIZATION

At the other extreme from the Malaysian solution is legalization—removing the criminal penalties from drugs altogether. Supporters of legalization point out that making alcohol illegal in the 1920s didn't stop people from getting drunk. Nor did it end the social problems associated with alcoholism and drunkenness. In fact, they argue, it made them worse, by creating the vicious criminal organizations that ran the illegal liquor trade.

The government is making the same mistake with drugs it made with Prohibition, argues Eric Sterling, the president of the Criminal Justice Policy Foundation. He insists that the government's drug war is "simplistic." It "moves our nation's response to the drug problem in the wrong direction. Prohibition failed for alcohol, is failing for drugs—and will continue to fail."

Legalization appeals to a minority of people of many political views. Even some conservatives, like the Nobel Prize-winning economist Milton Friedman and columnist William Buckley, favor it. These conservatives see drug use as a matter of individual freedom. If an adult wants to take the personal risks involved in using drugs, they argue, he or she should have the right to do so. The government should not interfere.

Others favor legalization on more practical grounds. They claim, in Pat Buchanan's words, that legalizing drug use would "take the crime out of it." Judge Robert Sweet, for one, argues that it would eliminate "the profit motive, the gangs, [and] the drug dealers." That, in turn, would eliminate most of the violence now associated with the drug problem. Gangs would no longer fight for sales territory on the streets of our cities. Innocent people would no longer be caught in the crossfire.

In fact, supporters of legalization argue, there would be no need for drugs to be sold on the streets at all. They could be sold in pharmacies or in specialized stores licensed for the purpose. Sold legally, they could be regulated, the way alcohol is regulated today. Minors could still be forbidden to buy or use drugs. Drug use could still be banned on the job or when driving cars or other vehicles.

Since the price of legal drugs would be lower, fewer addicts would steal money to buy their drugs. What is more, legalization would eliminate most, if not all, of the political and police corruption associated with today's illegal drug trade.

According to its proponents, legalization would also have important economic benefits. The most immediate is the money that would be saved by ending the war on drugs. These savings, Judge Sweet argues, should be spent on combating "the source of this problem, which is poverty and disillusion." In addition, say the supporters, once they were made legal, drugs could be taxed. This would turn what is now a drain on the government's resources into a source of revenue. The opponents of legalization argue that this is unlikely. Any income the government would gain from taxing drugs, they say, it would have to spend to regulate them.

Even the supporters of legalization admit that it would not end the drug problem. It would not eliminate drug abuse, nor would it end the personal suffering and tragedy associated with drug addiction. It would not save a Len Bias from dying of a cocaine overdose, or a Lisa Steinberg from being beaten to death by a drug-abusing stepfather.

In fact, the opponents of legalization are convinced that it would cause even more such tragedies to occur. They argue that many more people would experiment with drugs if they were legal. And, as a direct result, many more people would become addicted. William Von Raub, who headed one front in the drug war for the Reagan administration, warns that legalization could result in 4 to 5 million new cocaine addicts. Dr. Herbert Kleber of Yale Medical School puts the potential many times higher. Supporters of legalization scoff at these predictions. They say they are based on the assumption that virtually everyone would try drugs if they were legal. Since it is well known that the drugs in question are dangerous, they say, most people would never try them. Of those who did, the great majority would not become addicted.

All other arguments aside, however, the opponents object to legalization primarily on moral grounds. As William Bennett said of the Bush administration's drug policies, "The basic premise...is that drug use is *wrong*." Bennett and the other opponents of legalization believe that making drugs legal would mean denying that premise. Worst of all, they say, it would mean sending "the wrong message" to young people. By making drug use *legally* acceptable, they argue, the government would be suggesting that it is *morally* acceptable as well.

Most supporters of legalization would agree that drug abuse is morally wrong. But, they insist, the evils that result from keeping drugs illegal are even worse than those that would come from lifting the restrictions. Their view was expressed by Virginia Postrel, editor of *Reason* magazine, in an editorial in *USA Today*: "The prohibitionists substitute law for morality," she argued. "Legalizing drugs would put issues of morality back where they belong—in the churches, the families, the private realm."

Ultimately, it is unlikely that either of the extreme alternatives will be adopted in the United States. Neither the Malaysian

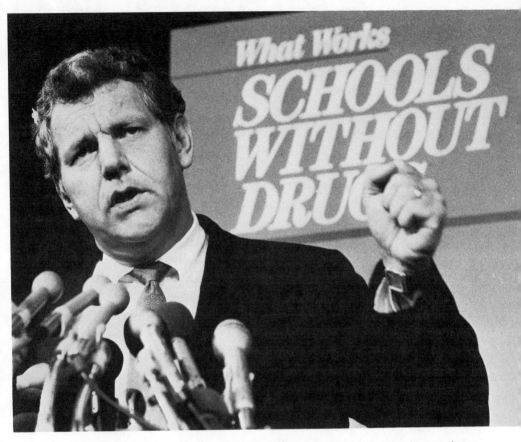

William Bennett, the Bush administration's "drug czar," emphasizes the importance of fighting drug abuse in the nation's schools.

solution nor legalization has widespread support, either in
Congress or among the public at large.

So the drug war will go on. What are the prospects for that
war? Will it succeed? William Bennett thinks it is succeeding
already. "The line has been drawn," he says. "And I believe the
worst is over. We aren't there yet...but we know where we're
going and we know how to get there."

On the other hand, critics like Michigan's Representative
John Conyers argue that, because it ignores the underlying social
problems, the drug war is bound to fail. Meanwhile, more
conservative critics like Pat Buchanan complain that it is a "no-

win war," and insist "the idea that we're going to solve this problem in the next four years is ludicrous."

One thing all sides agree on is that, as Senator Joseph Biden of Delaware has said, "The single most significant weapon we have in this drug war...is the moral approbation of society." Drug use soared in the 1960s, when whole segments of society began to accept it as a fact of everyday life. If it is to decline in the 1990s, it will be because more and more Americans, in all parts of society, reject it as socially and morally unacceptable.

There are signs that this is beginning to happen. In several cities, angry citizens are reclaiming streets that had once been taken over by drug dealers. Social and religious groups, such as the Nation of Islam (Black Muslims), are leading the fight in many neighborhoods. In others, it is individual citizens, like Barbara White of Philadelphia, whose seven-year-old grandson was partially paralyzed by a drug dealer's bullet. Now she goes out with her neighbors to confront the drug dealers and force them off their chosen street corners. In one night, she boasts, they cost the drug dealers of Philadelphia half a million dollars.

A middle-aged woman named Georgette Watson helps run a program called Drop-a-Dime/Report-Crime in the Roxbury neighborhood of Boston. People who learn about drug deals, or other crimes, can call anonymously to tip off the police. About 600 people do call every month, and many drug dealers are arrested as a result. Groups in other cities have started to copy the Boston program.

Most encouraging of all is the evidence that drug use is becoming less and less attractive to young people. Fewer high school students are experimenting with cocaine than at any time in years. And, as William Bennett told Senator Biden's Judiciary Committee, "even college freshmen...are very conservative on the issue of drug use."

"All across this country," the drug czar testified, "Americans are saying that they will no longer tolerate the use of illegal drugs, not at home, not at work, not in their neighborhoods."

If that is so, there is hope for the drug war yet.

BIBLIOGRAPHY

BOOKS

Blumenthal, Ralph. *Last Days of the Sicilians: the FBI's War Against tʰ Mafia* (New York: Pocket Books, 1988).

Daley, Robert. *Prince of the City: the True Story of a Cop Who Knew Too Much* (Boston: Houghton Mifflin, 1978).

Eddy, Paul, with Hugo Sabogal and Sara Walden. *The Cocaine Wars.* (New York: Bantam, 1988).

Kempe, Frederick. *Divorcing the Dictator.* (New York: G.P. Putnam's Sons, 1990).

McCoy, Al, et. al. *The Politics of Heroin in Southeast Asia.* (New York: Harper & Row, 1972).

Mills, James. *The Underground Empire.* (Garden City, N.Y.: Doubleday, 1986).

Moore, Robin. *The French Connection.* (Boston: Little, Brown, 1969).

Shannon, Elaine. *Desperados* (New York: Penguin, 1989).

ARTICLES

"Children of the Underclass," by Tom Morganthau and others, *Newsweek*, September 11, 1989.

"Coca: An Ancient Indian Herb Turns Deadly," by Peter T. White. *National Geographic*, January, 1989.

"Cocaine Billionaires," by Alan Riding, *New York Times Magazine*, March 8, 1987.

"Cocaine's 'Dirty 300,'" by Tom Morganthau and others, *Newsweek*, Nov. 13, 1989.

"Crack's Destructive Sprint Across America," by Michael Massing, *New York Times Magazine*, Oct. 1, 1989.

Debate—"Making Drugs Legal Won't Win the War," by editors, and "Making Drugs Legal Will End So-Called War" by Virginia Postrel, *USA Today*, Dec. 15, 1989.

"A Dirty Drug Secret," by Larry Martz, *Newsweek*, Feb. 19, 1990.

"Epidemiology of Drug Abuse: An Overview," by Nicholas J. Kozel and Edgar H. Adams, *Science*, Nov. 21, 1986.

"A Fair, Honorable, and Legitimate Trade," by Geoffrey C. Ward and Frederic Delano Grant, Jr., *American Heritage Magazine*, Aug.-Sept., 1986.

"The Fire of Ice," by Michael A. Lerner, *Newsweek*, November 27, 1989.

"Inside the High-Flying Pot Industry," by Gordon Witkin and Alice C. Cuneo, *U.S. News & World Report*, Nov. 6, 1989.

"Now It's Bush's War," by Tom Morganthau and others, *Newsweek*, September 18, 1989.

"A Plague Without Boundaries," by Philip Elmer-deWitt, and others, *Time*, Nov. 6, 1989.

"The Return of a Deadly Drug Called Horse," by Gordon Witkin, *U.S. News & World Report*, Aug. 14, 1989.

INDEX

Michael Kronenwetter is a freelance writer and journalist. *Drugs in America* is his thirteenth book for young adults. Two of the others—*The War on Terrorism* and *Managing Toxic Waste*—were also published by Julian Messner. In addition, Kronenwetter is the author of the award-winning filmstrip *America's Power and Prestige Since Vietnam,* as well as of many works for adults. These include a short story for the radio, a newspaper column about television, and a history of the region in which he was raised.

Kronenwetter lives in Wisconsin with his wife and two children.